Claire came down to earth with a wallop!

Dizzy with her success in getting Dane to agree to marry her, she hadn't considered Max and how furious he'd be about her scheme to marry Dane.

Dane wouldn't lose any sleep if she did back down—but how could she change her mind now?

If she went ahead, she and Max would eventually have a home together just as they'd always planned, with all the love and warmth in it she'd been denied here. If she didn't marry Dane, there would be no wedding, no future home. Max wouldn't take on a wife he had to support in his present situation.

Everything in her retreated from such an uncertain and depressing future. Max would have to understand that sometimes one just had to reach out and grab happiness in case a second chance never came....

Lynne Graham was born in Ireland and, at the age of fifteen, submitted her first romantic novel, unsuccessfully, to Mills & Boon. Just when she was planning a career in law, a Christmas visit home resulted in her having to make a choice between career or marriage to a man she had loved since her teens. They live in Ireland in a household overflowing with dogs, plants and books. When their now seven-year-old daughter was a toddler, Lynne began writing again, this time with success.

Bittersweet Passion

Lynne Graham

Harlequin Books

TORONTO • NEW YORK • LONDON
AMSTERDAM • PARIS • SYDNEY • HAMBURG
STOCKHOLM • ATHENS • TOKYO • MILAN

Original hardcover edition published in 1987
by Mills & Boon Limited

ISBN 0-373-17015-7

Harlequin Romance first edition June 1988

CHAPTER ONE

'GOOD God!' Steve whispered irreverently. 'Dane's actually come.'

A perceptible flutter of interest spread through the gathered mourners at Adam Fletcher's graveside. Several pairs of eyes wearing expressions ranging from curiosity to outright disapproval watched the approach of the prodigal as he strode across the cemetery. The lugubrious vicar cleared his throat and glanced enquiringly at the slender girl by his side.

'I think we'd better wait,' she agreed quietly.

On her other side Carter Fletcher's thin face set into angry lines. 'How did he find out?' he muttered.

Claire's cheekbones washed with pink, since she had been the one to see that Dane was informed. As his tall, carelessly dressed figure drew level she lowered her eyes.

When Dane's mother, Adam's only daughter, had married not only a foreigner but a man who had made his fortune in casinos, nightclubs and what were euphemistically termed girlie magazines, Adam Fletcher had struck her name from the family Bible. Shortly after her death, however, he had chosen to acknowledge Dane's existence by inviting him up to Ranbury Hall for the weekend. Not that Dane, by then having reached twenty-one, had shown himself properly grateful for such belated attention. Already rich beyond avarice, Dane had come out of curiosity alone, and unlike the rest of Adam's family, he had never toadied.

'Man that is born of woman . . .' The sepulchral voice intoned.

Claire swallowed hard. Not a single soul present truly mourned her grandfather's death. An eccentric, miserly and reclusive old man, he had been no more polite or pleasant to his neighbours than he had been to his own immediate family.

Claire's father had been Adam's youngest and least successful son. Her parents had led a somewhat gipsyish existence because her father had rarely stuck in one job for long. She had been four when they had adopted her, and her memory of the six years she had had with them was a warm cocoon to retire inside whenever she was low. Money had been in short supply but there had been love. Their sudden death in a car crash had cut unimaginably deep, and her life at Ranbury Hall afterwards had been achingly familiar. Before her adoption she had been in a variety of foster homes and institutions. There, too, there had often been coldness and disinterest, a sense of not belonging to anything or anybody, and that buried insecurity had been fanned to a flame from the moment she arrived at Ranbury to make her home with Adam Fletcher.

'The law may say you're my granddaughter but we both know you're not,' he had growled resentfully. 'You were adopted. You're no kin of mine but I can't have it said I let you go into an institution. I expect you'll be able to make yourself useful about the house. You're not a pretty child, either. I dare say you'll still be here when I'm doddering and needing a nurse.'

In the chilly breeze gusting across the exposed grave-yard, she shivered beneath her thin navy raincoat. Adam had been correct in his forecast. She was twenty-three now and, apart from a few years in a boarding school outside Leeds, she had been no further than Ranbury and its overgrown acres in the Yorkshire Dales. But a year ago, a year that was now etched into her soul as a timeless, agonising period of unhappiness, she could have gone to the man she loved, had not Adam's illness made it impossible for her to leave.

In staying she had done what everyone estimated to be her duty, and four days ago Adam had passed away in his sleep. There was no longer any reason for her to remain at Ranbury. Max had waited patiently for over a year for her to join him in London. Soon she would have a new life, a new beginning with someone who wanted her for herself . . . someone who cared about her as a person with feelings and needs of her own. That had to be a first in Claire's experience.

Her grandfather had found her an unwelcome responsibility until he saw how useful a quiet, hard-working girl could be around a large, understaffed house and what savings could be made through that same girl's painstaking efforts to budget. And, of late, she'd been much cheaper than a private nurse. A nurse wouldn't have stood Adam's sharp, vindictive tongue, the barrage of constant, nagging complaints that had made Claire's days unendurable. All the compassion in the world could prove insufficient when life became one long, unremitting toil ruled by the whims of a cold, tyrannical old man.

It's over now, a little voice soothed inside her brain. Tiredly she lifted her auburn head again, ashamed of such unforgiving thoughts. After all, she was free now to make her own choices and her choice was quite naturally to be reunited with Max. Thankfully no one could prevent that now.

'Ashes to ashes, dust to dust . . .' Carter's arm curved firmly to her waist and she stiffened in taut rejection of his familiarity.

Opposite, her gaze collided unexpectedly with Dane's chillingly beautiful, bright blue eyes and the tinge of amusement in the faint tilt of his mouth. Reddening, she looked away again. At least she could absolve Dane of paying his respects only out of a desire to see what his grandfather had left him. Dane was much wealthier than ever the Fletchers had been and he hailed from a very different world.

The depth of his tan emphasised the amount of time he spent abroad and the tight-fitting black cords and designer-cut leather jerkin he sported were not, she imagined, the mark of disrespect Carter's face so clearly said they were, but more likely to be a sign that Dane had flown back in a hurry and probably from the States to attend the funeral. Even so, she had never seen him in a suit. Raised in California, even though he now based the headquarters of the Visconti business interests in London, Dane was a great deal less hidebound and conventional than his cousins.

'Miss Fletcher.' The vicar was shaking her hand first because she alone of the assembled group had lived with the departed.

'Claire.' Dane's hand engulfed hers firmly. 'My condolences. Was it sudden?'

Her witch-hazel eyes widened behind her tortoiseshell spectacles. 'No, he was ill for a long time,' she murmured. 'It was a release for him to die.'

'You shouldn't have said that,' Carter sniped, pressing her back on to the gravel path. 'It sounded disrespectful.' Then, 'Dane had no business coming here.'

'I'm glad he came,' she countered. 'I always thought Grandfather had a soft spot for him, even though he'd never have admitted it.'

'Nonsense, Claire.' Carter made a minute adjustment to his tie as they headed towards the cars waiting beyond the wall. 'Far be it from me to boast, but I was always the favourite.'

Lord, what a petty little man he was ! Arriving too late to make the funeral arrangements, he had none the less managed to question each and every one of them. When Steve, her other cousin, ignored his parents' car and climbed in behind Carter, she smiled relief. Still a student, Steve had done little but regale her with descriptions of his fiancée and apologise for his few visits of recent. But then, who could say Ranbury Hall was inviting? she reflected wryly. Her grandfather had not expended a penny on the rambling property during the past fifty years. The amount of comfort available there was marginal.

'Look at the car Dane's travelling in!' Steve nearly broke his neck peering out at the long, opulent limousine with its tinted windows, which was parked at the end of the church lane. 'My mother must be going green with envy!'

Carter delivered him a scornful glance. 'Did Celia inform Dane of Adam's death?' he demanded, Celia being Carter's aunt and Steve's mother.

Claire chewed her lip uneasily. 'No, that was me, Carter.'

He looked at her in astonishment 'You?' he parroted.

'He had a right to be told,' she stated levelly, though her cheeks were pale. 'I contacted his secretary in London. She didn't tell me where he was. Actually, at the time I didn't think she paid much heed to my message. I had enough trouble just getting to speak to her.'

Steve laughed, understanding. 'I doubt if Dane ever felt the need to name-drop grandfather's existence.'

Carter was still staring at her, flushed by angry incredulity. 'You should have discussed it with me first. Dane hasn't been up here in years.'

'Three years,' Claire inserted. 'And you know Grand-

father told him not to come again. He was very rude to him
on that last visit.'

'No ruder than he ever was to anyone else.' Carter let
down his sanctimonious front to stab, 'To attend his funeral
now is the height of bad taste and, if Dane's expecting to
find any profit for himself out of the reading of the will,
he'll soon find his mistake.'

Her distaste threatened to choke her. Aside of the last
couple of months when it had been clear that Adam
Fletcher was on his deathbed, Carter had been a very
infrequent visitor here. Once he had reached that
realisation he had visited regularly, showing a calculation
Claire had despised. It had not been lost on her, either, that
her grandfather had belatedly reached the conclusion that
Carter would make her an excellent husband. Stolid and
careful in his ways, and equally penny-pinching, Carter
had managed to impress Adam deeply.

She was glad when the car glided through the tall, rusty
gates and came to a halt on the weedy gravel fronting the
granite bareness of the Hall. Hard winters had scarred the
paintwork, neglect had done the rest and on a prematurely
dark, wintry afternoon, the Hall proffered a gloomy
welcome.

Seeing Mr Coverdale's stately old Rover already parked,
she hastened from the car. 'I'll see that some tea is served
first. It's bitterly cold.'

In her opinion the will would contain no surprises. The
estate would be divided equally between all of them. For
what reason other than that belief would Carter have asked
her to marry him a mere week ago? As she passed the hall
mirror her own colourless and drab exterior mocked her.

She had not grown up pretty. Those teenage fantasies
had died years ago. She was short-sighted, undersized and,
at any gathering, likely to be the one offering the

refreshments around. Carter was too grasping to have proposed without the conviction that she would bring with her a sizeable dowry.

Money! A bitter smile crossed her small face. She glanced at threadbare curtains and worn carpets, furniture that had never been anything other than cheap and functional even in its day. There was no heating. The hot water supply was unreliable and the kitchens prehistoric. Precious little enjoyment her grandfather had taken from his money!

A year ago Claire had been naïvely happy. Max Walker, the trainee estate manager at Ranbury, had asked her to marry him. Her shyness and reserve briefly forgotten, she had flown straight to her grandfather to tell him. Adam had sacked Max and, before she could pack her bags and follow, Adam had not only informed her that he had cancer but that if she disobeyed him he would dispense with the elderly servants still in his employ. The threat of unhousing Maisie and Sam Morley, who lived in a tumbledown cottage on the edge of the estate had horrified her. Nor had it been necessary.

Duty was a yoke that Claire had never shirked and she had done everything possible to ease her grandfather's last months alive. She had also sought to persuade him to make some small provision in his will for the old couple who, as housekeeper and gardener, had worked for him throughout his life. But since he had considered them the Social Service's responsibility to house and keep, she had small hope that his attitude would have softened.

Hanging her coat, she hurried into the kitchen. Maisie took one look at her tense, wan face and abandoning the tea trolley enveloped Claire in a warm, reassuring hug. 'It's done now and everything will come all right,' the old lady promised kindly. 'And don't you let anyone bully you into thinking otherwise.'

Claire blinked back tears. She had been dry-eyed all day. But Maisie's rough affection touched her to the heart, for the old housekeeper had to be concerned about her own future. She was in her seventies, with an ailing and not very mobile husband, and accommodation that was tied to her job. She had much more to worry about.

'Yes, everything's going to be fine.' There was a calm quality to Claire's voice as she pulled herself firmly together. Adam was bound to have left her enough money to ensure that the Morleys' remaining years were comfortable ones. The family had always talked as if he was loaded. A pension, she planned absently, and that little house—such as it was—signed over to them. It might even be possible to have the cottage refurbished.

Some of her tension drained away as she thought daringly of her own plans. In the heat of a long ago summer's day, Max had shyly confided that his dearest ambition was to have a farm of his own. Since neither of them had had any money, it had seemed just a dream. But now Claire wondered dizzily just how much a small piece of land and a modest house could cost. They'd be able to get married immediately instead of waiting—Max was still without a job. He wouldn't need one if he had land of his own to work. Things might be tight but that was nothing she wasn't used to . . . and they'd be together as two people in love ought to be together. Not subsisting on a diet of unsatisfactory letters to keep their relationship alive. Poor Max, he found letters such a labour. She still treasured each and every one of his missives, though they mainly catalogued his daily doings and his frustration with inactivity.

'Claire!' Carter snapped. 'Mr Coverdale's waiting.'

Her eyes gleamed with annoyance as Maisie guiltily returned to making the tea.

'She's only the housekeeper. I wish you'd remember that,' Carter complained as she followed him. 'You're much too familiar with her.'

Prevented by the presence of others from an angry and unashamed rebuttal, she contented herself with the reflection that Carter's snobbery scarcely mattered now. It would be a relief, not a hardship for Maisie to retire. Apart from Claire, none of the Fletchers had ever cherished the smallest warmth towards her. If there was anything the family respected apart from the great god Money, it was the dividing line between family and hired help. Claire had always straddled the borderline between. Oh, she was a Fletcher now when Carter considered her worthy of a marriage proposal, but for long years she had just been Adam's unwanted ward who helped around the house. Carter must think she had an incredibly short memory!

Her grandfather's solicitor, a small man in his late fifties, came forward to greet her, apologising for his unavoidable absence from the funeral. Steve and his parents, James and Celia were already standing close to the miserable fire flickering in the large drawing-room grate. Carter's older sister, Sandra, who had kept house for him since the death of their parents, was already seated. Dane strolled in last, and she remembered abruptly that he hated tea and sped past him to head for the kitchen again.

Although Adam had raved in his moments of religious fervour about Dane's notorious reputation and jet-set life-style, Claire could dimly recall occasions during her unhappy childhood here when Dane had been carelessly kind to her. Indeed, when she had been sixteen she had developed a quite hopeless crush on Dane who, to her adolescent eyes, represented every woman's fantasy. She

was rather glad he hadn't noticed it. Not that she had
flaunted her feelings. Her wayward emotions had made her
more tongue-tied and self-conscious than ever and in any
case, she had nurtured no fantasies on wish-fulfilment.

Dane was one of the Beautiful People, fêted in the gossip
columns and the subject of many a risqué kiss'n'tell story by
discarded exes, recountals in Sunday newspapers that
Claire had once been avidly glued to. Even then the mere
concept of Dane even registering that she was female had
amused her.

'Where are you bolting off to now?' His lazy enquiry was
accompanied by a restraining hand on her sleeve. 'Go and
sit down. You look exhausted.'

And could have done without being told so. She stole a
rueful glance up at his strikingly handsome features, the
silvery-blond hair luxuriantly curving over his collar in
such effective contrast to the winged ebony brows and
spiky lashes he had inherited from his Italian father. It was
an arrogant face, his strength of character underwritten by
his superb bone structure. The long, narrow-bridged
perfection of his nose lent decided *hauteur* to his features,
and cynicism and sensuality combined in the hard,
chiselled line of his mouth. He was quite breathtakingly
good-looking. Little wonder that he went through women
like a fox in a hen-yard, she allowed grudgingly.

'I'll be back in a moment.' Circumspectly she dragged
her eyes from him. What did he see? Poor, bullied, plain
spinster cousin Claire? He would be surprised how much
purpose seethed beneath her composed exterior. Even more
surprised perhaps to learn there was a man in her life.

'Coffee for Dane, Maisie!' she called into the kitchen.

'Claire!' Carter erupted afresh, somewhere in her wake.

She hastened back, rather flushed and harassed, to take
a seat in one of the hard, overstuffed armchairs. Mr

Coverdale was unfurling papers from his briefcase.
'Firstly—' he cast a rather wary glance round the room
'—there are people present who do not benefit from Mr
Fletcher's last will and testament.'

'We're all family,' Carter said loftily. 'Please continue.'

The older man sighed. 'Mr Fletcher had for some time
intended that Miss Claire Fletcher be the sole beneficiary of
his estate, but a year ago he made alterations to his will. I
did seek to reason with him about the terms he included,
but to no avail, and I feel it my duty to inform you, Miss
Fletcher, that . . .'

'The sole beneficiary? The sole beneficiary?' Celia was
repeating furiously.

An expression of rich enjoyment crossed Dane's faintly
bored features and he lowered himself down gracefully into
a chair near the window, his air one of strong anticipation.

'That it is very unlikely that you could combat those
terms in court,' Mr Coverdale completed.

'She's getting everything?' Celia ranted, still not over the
first statement, her plump face a blotchy pink.

Carter curled his lip over his aunt's annoyance. 'And
who more deserving, Celia? Claire was a very dutiful
granddaughter. I'm sure no one could argue that anyone
else was more entitled. If you listen, however, you will
realise that Grandfather didn't make the bequest without
qualification.'

Under the loud backlash of family comment, Claire had
paled. A year ago the will had been changed. Her romance
with Max had shaken her grandfather up more than he had
admitted. She wasn't disapppointed. In fact, she was
grateful not to have received the entire estate. She could
hardly feel it was her due. As long as there was still enough
for the Morleys, she told herself squarely, and mentally
crossed her fingers.

'Unfortunately Mr Fletcher's affairs are in quite a tangle
and I don't yet have adequate valuations on the investments my client made out in South Africa. He mortgaged
this house to do so. However, I can tell you that—' the
solicitor advanced, affecting not to hear the gasps of
surprise '—the money does rest in those investments and I
imagine that the amount will be a considerable one. Now I
shall read the will, if I may.'

Taken aback by the news that the Hall was mortgaged,
Claire resolutely attempted to avoid Carter's meaningful
smile in her direction. He seemed expectant, excited
almost, as though the contents of the will were already
known to him.

'... being of sound mind do bequeath my estate in its
entirety to my granddaughter, Claire, on the condition that
she marries one of my grandsons, such choice being an
obvious one ... He did insist on writing this himself,' Mr
Coverdale murmured uncomfortably, as if the unearthly
silence that had fallen and Claire's shocked stillness had
penetrated even his bland good humour. 'You see, he
believed it would take a man to run his business affairs,
Miss Fletcher, but Mr Carter Fletcher assured me that you
were only holding off from a formal announcement out of
respect for you grandfather's demise. Or am I premature in
mentioning the matter?'

Shattered by Carter's unforgivable machinations to line
his own pockets, Claire was incapable of speech.

'Congratulations.' Sandra kissed her cheek with newly
discovered cousinly affection. 'It's by far the fairest
arrangement.'

Claire's teeth sank into the soft underside of her lower lip
and she tasted blood. 'It's iniquitious ... humiliating ...'
Her stifled voice wasted away.

'Claire, you're overwrought.' A heavy hand came down to pat her shoulder.

Instinctively she flinched from Carter's proprietorial hold, too disgusted even to look at him. Well, his visits to their grandfather had certainly paid good dividends! 'What happens if I don't marry Carter?' she asked.

The solicitor looked distinctly uneasy. 'The will doesn't specify which of your male cousins,' he added as if he believed this might be of some help to her.

'I'm engaged!' Steve burst out abruptly.

Dane gave up the ghost and laughed with unholy amusement.

Celia rounded on him like a tigress. 'It's all very well for you to laugh,' she snapped. 'The money means nothing to you!'

Dane dealt her a sardonic smile. 'Was that your Roller or someone else's I saw at the cemetery? Good God, none of you are broke except Claire,' he breathed contemptuously.

'I shall continue now,' Mr Coverdale cut in hurriedly before hostilities escalated afresh. 'There is a small bequest and . . . an alternative. To my grandson Dane, I bequeath my Bible.' A pindropping silence fell. 'To James and Celia, nothing because . . .' He hesitated fatally.

'Nothing?' Celia screeched incredulously. 'Because of what?'

The solicitor breathed in like a man girding his loins. 'Because during my lifetime I on several occasions advanced certain monies to my son James, which he did not repay although I did remind him of the debts . . .'

'Come, James.' Celia arose majestically. 'Steven! We're not staying here any longer.'

'And in the event of my granddaughter Claire pursuing that relationship which I did not approve of and no marriage taking place with my grandson, my estate, is to be sold and the proceeds given to the Temperance Society.'

'Who shall I serve first?' Maisie asked as she noisily wheeled in the tea trolley.

Carter cleared his throat. 'What relationship, Claire?'

She got up quickly. 'I believe that's my business, Carter. Please excuse me for a moment, Mr Coverdale,' she murmured and followed her aunt and uncle's sweeping departure to the hall.

Steve clasped her hand, his boyish face wreathed with embarrassment. 'I'm sorry, I didn't mean ...' he began awkwardly.

'I didn't take offence.' She forced a smile because she liked him. Clearly Celia's behaviour had mortified him. How often had Adam embarrassed her in front of others? Once too often today, she thought, going down the steps to speak to her aunt and uncle.

'Oh, it's not your fault,' Celia was saying petulantly to her hen-pecked husband. 'I hated him. He was a miserable, cantankerous old goat and I don't care if he was your father, James! I never had a polite word from him.'

'Won't you stay to dinner?' Claire pressed unhappily.

Celia spun on her diminutive niece. 'You have to be joking,' she said cuttingly. 'I wish you joy with Carter. He's an Adam in the making!'

Her uncle squeezed her hand apologetically. 'She doesn't mean it, you know. Carter's a fine young man.'

She watched them depart and then found Mr Coverdale already hovering in the hall behind her. 'I had finished, Miss Fletcher. If you have any queries, please don't hesitate to call.'

'He left nothing for the staff here?' In her anxiety she double-checked.

'Unfortunately not. I'm afraid my client was not of a benevolent disposition,' he said heavily.

What an understatement! Still in shock, Claire glanced into the drawing-room where Carter and Sandra were in close confab. Dane was nowhere to be seen. She suspected him of taking refuge in the library. Striving to calm herself down, Claire went into the kitchen. But what on earth was she going to do?

Her grandfather had removed her from school at sixteen. She had no training for any career. She hadn't even got to sit her O-levels. Maisie was sitting tiredly by the kitchen table. Claire looked away again, a terrible bitterness consuming her as she tasted the full portent of her grandfather's selfishness. She did not have a penny of her own to give the Morleys. Would ceding them that pitiful cottage for the remainder of their lives have been such a sacrifice? How mightily self-satisfied he must have been after penning that will to explode upon all of them but Carter.

She dragged out the vegetable basket and piled potatoes into the sink. It was after five. She might as well start dinner early.

'Here. I got it from my car.' A liqueur glass landed on the edge of the draining board. Dane gave her a mocking smile. 'You need a drink more than you need a cup of half-cold tea. Are you all set to celebrate your nuptials with Carter?'

His amusement struck her as cruel. Yes, in a sense Celia had spoken truly. Dane didn't have a clue what it felt like to be a charity case or to be humiliated as she had been by that will. Her grandfather had literally proffered a bribe to Carter to marry her.

'No.'

He lounged with indolent grace back against the old wooden cupboards. 'Then you're going to pursue the unsuitable relationship?' he guessed. 'You surprise me. I never thought you had the guts to rebel.'

Her cheeks flamed. 'You're very frank.'

He shrugged indifferently. 'I came to tell you I'd give you a lift down to London if you want one, and I'll fix you up with somewhere to stay,' he offered casually. 'Knowing Adam, you haven't even got the price of your next meal.'

She lifted the potato peeler and resisted an urge to dig it into his lean, muscular ribcage. If only it were that easy. Her hopes had been dashed to smithereens. She had foolishly dared to dream and by doing so had tripled her own disappointment. When was she going to learn? The thought train verged too close to self-pity and she killed it stone dead. There would be no farm for Max, no home that she could finally call her own. Thanks to Adam, Max was on the dole queue, sacked without a reference because he had dared to offer her marriage and that hadn't fitted in with Adam's plans.

How could she go to Max now, penniless, with only a few shabby clothes to her name? What prospect did she even have of supporting herself? She had no qualifications, no marketable talent outside the domestic sphere. She would be a millstone round Max's neck.

Yet for so long she had dreamt of making Max's dream come true and sharing that dream with him. Rigid with self-discipline, totally unaware of Dane's sharply assessing scrutiny, she noticed Maisie quietly tidying up in the pantry, and her selfish absorption in her own predicament left a nasty taste in her mouth. At least she had health and youth on her side. The Morleys had only the expectancy that a lifetime of service would lead to an easier old age. And now even that was to be denied them

Carter's peevish voice sprung her from her depressing introspection. 'What are you drinking, Claire?'

Dane expelled his breath. 'Oh, put the lid on it, Carter. You were always a dead bore. You don't need to labour the point the way you do,' he drawled.

Ignoring Carter, Claire glanced hopefully at Dane. 'You'll stay to dinner?' she urged. 'It won't be anything special, of course, but . . .'

'Shall I send my chauffeur out for some steak?' Dane interposed calmly. 'We could all do with a decent meal. I'll go and tell him.'

Carter's mouth worked convulsively as Dane breezed past him. 'Who does he think he is?' he finally managed.

'He was being practical,' she countered with unwitting defensiveness. 'He knows what the housekeeping budget is like here and I assume he's hungry.'

'I wasn't talking about Dane's appetite!' he parried shortly.

Claire continued doggedly to peel potatoes. 'I didn't suppose you were, Carter, but I really don't have anything else to discuss with you,' she stressed coldly.

Impervious to hints, he murmured with an air of self-restraint. 'I'll speak to you later.'

Claire managed to smile at Maisie. 'I think it's time you went home. You must be exhausted. I can manage fine.'

Alone then, she pictured a life sentence of Carter and abandoned the picture with a shiver. The assiduous toadying with which he had paved his every visit here to Adam had made her stomach heave. Now resentment hurtled fiercely through her in addition. The will doesn't specify which of your cousins. The solicitor's deadpan aside produced a humourless smile on her mouth. As if she was ready to barter herself to anyone for money! Unless it wasn't a real marriage . . . the insidious thought crept in. In an illuminating flash she saw the possibility of solving all her problems in one fell swoop.

Maisie and Sam would be secure. She could be with Max without being a burden. No, it was a fantastic notion, born out of sheer despair, and there was only one possible candidate. Dane. He was Adam's grandson, too. But Dane would think she was crazy. The idea of even approaching him on such a mission plunged her sharply back to cold reality.

She flushed guiltily when he reappeared to dump a carrier bag on the table. 'I like beef Stroganoff,' he informed her, oblivious to her blushes as he departed again.

Dane always spoke with the assurance and habit of command. Even in his normal garb of jeans, the aura of power and unspoken expectations clung to him. But then from birth Dane had had everything he wanted. He was bound to be pretty selfish and spoilt by the fashion in which women pursued him. Her weary mouth down-curved. Who the heck did he think was going to toil over a hot stove to make his wretched meal? But why should he think? Used as he was to servants, it would not occur to Dane that he was creating hassle she could well do without.

The atmosphere round the table in the icy cold dining-room was tense. Dane ate with unblemished appetite. Carter, who looked upon anything remotely different in the food line as suspicious, poked his food round his plate, and Sandra was too busy trying to flirt with Dane to notice what she was eating.

'Is it OK if I stay tonight?' Dane enquired lazily. 'I'm jet-lagged and I don't feel like another journey.'

Claire nodded politely. 'That's fine.'

Another two beds to make up, unless he expected his chauffeur to sleep in the car! She trailed worn, thin sheets from the airing cupboard and trekked into the bedrooms. The rooms were so cold her breath was fogging in the air, and she went downstairs again to fill hot-water bottles that would take the chill off the rarely used beds. Then she lit a fire in Dane's room. He was sure to be finding it colder than anyone else.

By the time she had done all that and embarked on the dishes, she was practically asleep standing up. When Carter came in and demanded to know where Maisie was, she nearly screamed at him. Slowly she counted to ten. 'It's late, Carter. I sent her home hours ago.'

'Leave those, then. It's time we talked.'

Setting the last dish to drain, she dried her hands. 'Sorry, I'm going up to bed. It's been a very long day.'

His mouth narrowed in exasperation. 'For everybody, Claire,' he rebuked condescendingly.

A fuse blew, Claire planted her hands on her hips. 'Has it been? Were any of the rest of you involved in making beds, cleaning this wretched house or making meals? Has one of you so much as lifted a finger? Sandra and you arrived two days ago, and neither of you have done a single thing,' she condemned. 'Who do you think has been doing it? The fairies? The past week has been one long, relentless slog for me. I haven't been sitting around sipping tea. I've been serving it. I wouldn't marry you either, Carter, not if you went down on your bended knees and begged. I'm sorry your little plan has failed at the last ditch,' she lied in a shaking voice. 'Goodnight, Carter.'

She swept past his turkey-red face and mounted the stairs, hearing his shocked murmurings to his sister in the hall below. Well, she wasn't ashamed of herself! Whatever the future held for her, she wasn't going to be used by anyone again!

She recalled the social worker who had ferried her up here thirteen years ago. 'You're a very lucky little girl,' that lady had said innocently. 'You still have a family and you're going to live in a lovely big house. I expect you'll have lots of fun there.' And Claire could still remember the

coldness of the non-existent welcome mat, the lady's
uneasy, almost guilty departure.

On the surface, the passage of time had changed very
little. However, she was a grown woman now, not a
frightened, dependent child and if she didn't fight, no one
else would do the fighting for her, Automatically she
readied herself for bed.

'You'll be taken care of. I've seen to that,' Adam had
pronounced piously weeks ago.

Taken care of? By what right had he chosen to reach out
from beyond the grave to demand that she marry a man
who didn't even have the saving grace of respecting her?
And she owed Carter nothing. Neither he nor his sister had
even tried to ease the burden of nursing their grandfather.
But oh, yes! they all had time to attend the funeral and none
of them had the smallest interest in what happened to the
Morleys. For the first time she appreciated that Maisie and
Sam's future was dependent on what she herself chose to do
and the lunatic idea that had occurred to her earlier
suddenly didn't seem quite so fantastic any more.

Her hands shook with suppressed rage as she buttoned
her robe. After all these years was she to let the Morleys go
from this house penniless? Things might have been
different had she been allowed to train as a secretary . . . or
something. She could have helped them financially then.
Instead, she had spent the past seven years being nothing
more than a glorified servant. God knows, there weren't
even jobs out there for qualified people—what hope did she
have? And Max? Being fired hadn't helped his prospects.
He'd done nothing to deserve such treatment. Neither had
Maisie and Sam. Adam owed all of them more than that. If
she married Dane, the terms of the will would be fulfilled. It
would cost him nothing, yet it would mean so much to
everyone else concerned.

What harm would it do just to mention the idea to him? You're a coward. She glowered at herself myopically in the mirror. You could at least try. So what if he laughs? When are you likely to see him again?

Buoyed by a courage that was three-quarters desperation, she left her room and crept down the corridor to knock on Dane's door. His quiet answer encouraged her in.

To her dismay he was already in bed, lying back against the pillows like a rather gorgeous sleek and tawny tiger, replete, the covers dipping dangerously low on his flat stomach. A curling mass of dark hair covered a triangular V on his muscular chest and then tapered down to an intriguing silky furrow below his waist. Framed against the white sheets, his golden skin was all the more noticeable. The interior of her mouth ran dry and she hastily averted her eyes.

He smiled. 'I was just about to put out the light. Tell me, did everyone else qualify for a fire?'

Claire blushed and glanced at the fire she had kindled earlier. 'No, but since you're just back from abroad I thought you might feel the cold more. I need to speak to you ... could you put something on?' she asked hesitantly.

He laughed. 'Don't be such a prude, Claire. I don't have pyjamas, and I distinctly recall you spending half the night with me when you had toothache years ago. It didn't bother you then.'

'I was eleven.' Her breath was snarling up in her throat and she could feel her courage fleeing her second by second, so although she hadn't planned it that way, she just hurled it at him.' Dane ... will you marry me?'

CHAPTER TWO

IF she had ever desired to see Dane the unshockable shocked, she saw it now. Sapphire-blue eyes arrowed over her incredulously. 'Christ, you're not still hung up on me, are you?'

Her small hands dug into the pockets of her dressing-gown. How conceited could a man get? So he had noticed. She supposed she ought to be thanking her lucky stars that he hadn't felt the need to crush her with his cruel sarcasm back then.

'Naturally not,' she fielded stiltedly, wishing she had not gone too far to retreat. 'I'm in a fix or I wouldn't ask you. I'm not talking about a proper marriage, for goodness' sake. I don't know why you're looking at me like that! I only need a licence to satisfy grandfather's will.'

Dane pulled himself semi-upright in the bed and fixed his unsettling gaze on her tiny figure in the homespun dressing-gown, her slippered feet showing beneath the hem. 'Underneath, you're a real Fletcher, aren't you? Anything for money,' he derided. 'I just never figured you would have the colossal impertinence to even consider me! Stick to Carter.'

A tide of painful heat scorched her skin. But she could not leave him with the false impression he had. 'The Morleys will be in a terrible situation if there's no money . . .'

Dane surveyed her grimly. 'And who the hell are they?'

She thrust up her chin. 'Grandfather's two surviving servants. Sam is the gardener. He's not very well at the moment. Maisie's the housekeeper. They're both in their seventies. No, it's not funny, Dane.' Her husky voice

26

abruptly developed steel. 'They live in a cottage over at the Meadowfield. It's a hovel. Grandfather never did a single thing for them. If I don't marry someone, no one else is likely to help them.'

'You're breaking my heart,' he jibed softly. 'Couldn't you think up something more convincing than that?'

Valiantly she tamped down her anger. 'It's true, but apart from them . . . well . . . I'm in love . . .'

'With me?' he grated shortly. 'Go back to bed, Claire.'

'Damn you!' For the second time in the day, Claire lost her temper. 'There'd be something quite peculiar about me if I'd carried a teenage crush this long without encouragement! I'm in love with Max and he wants to marry me and I want to marry him,' she recited with relish. 'But I can't go to Max without a penny, Dane. It's not fair. I can't even get a decent job. And if you want to know, well I do resent the way I was taken from school before I even sat my exams. It left me fitted for nothing. One tiny sacrifice from you would settle all my problems.' Her voice had sunk down to a less forceful hiss as she ran out of steam.

Dane's appraisal was close to fascinated. His mobile mouth twitched. 'One tiny sacrifice?' he queried.

'Nobody outside the family would need to know,' she protested tightly. 'And I doubt if you have any deep-seated hang-ups about divorce.'

'I'm hanging on your every word,' he encouraged silkily. 'I never expected to be so diverted at Ranbury. It's been a truly amazing day.'

Claire interlinked her fingers tautly. 'It would be the perfect solution for everyone. The money could be divided up between all of us and then no one could be offended.'

'If you think Carter would thank you for a quarter when he's expecting the whole, you're a fool. And yes, you can absolve me of circumventing the will to get a share.'

His contempt was a new experience for Claire, but she

kept going. 'I have thought about that, and sometimes it's a matter of what's really right rather than paying dues to principles one can't afford . . .'

He swore half under his breath. 'Yes, you have thought about this.'

She flushed miserably. 'It's not any less ethical than Grandfather trying to force me into marriage with Carter, and it's certainly wrong that he made no provision for Maisie and Sam. But I quite see that since you don't get any profit out of it, it doesn't appeal.'

'Now that was below the belt,' he murmured.

Claire bit her lip. 'Perhaps, but I'm getting a little tired of being patronised, Dane.'

A winged ebony brow lifted with icy hauteur. 'Really?'

'Really!' She was trembling now. 'You think this is so damned amusing and so pathetically pushing of me, and you know very well I'm not like that. I wouldn't have mentioned it if there was any other choice! But you don't care what happens to those old people because they're not your responsibility, and you're acting insulted because I'm not the least pretty. I suppose it would have been less insulting if I had been,' she muttered tearfully. 'But I'd face anything before I had to face life with Carter, and I won't do it, which proves that wretched money isn't that important to me!'

She whirled out of the room before she could let her tongue make a bigger fool of herself. Why had she done it! Dane required neither the money nor the hassle, and if he had ever put himself out for anybody she had yet to hear of it. For all his scathing comments on Carter, she would not be surprised to discover that at the back of his mind Dane considered him a very fair match for her.

To give him his due, Carter had made no mention of love. He was not that big a liar. 'We get on well and we have tastes in common,' he had assumed in a rallying tone.

'And I don't need to tell you how pleased it would make Grandfather. But I see I've surprised you and I'm sure you want some time to think over the idea of marrying.' He had dealt her a smug, conceited smile. 'I expect you imagined you'd be staying single.'

She wondered bitterly if she might have considered such a loveless union had she not, through Max, realised how much more was available to her. Her desire for children might have tempted her. She saw again how devastated Dane had been, the insolent way his mouth had curled when she talked of loving Max, and she so wished Max had been here in the flesh to silence Carter. Had he been, she wouldn't have had to stupidly ask Dane for help. Dane didn't give a damn about things that didn't affect his comfort. She wiped her damp eyes crossly, deeply regretting the dignity she had abandoned with Dane.

'Claire ... wake up!' A firm hand was shaking her shoulder and her eyes flew open with a start, blinking at the light shining from the bedside lamp.

It was Dane standing over her, a sweater and a pair of jeans now covering him. 'What time is it?' she mumbled.

'Three, and I've been thinking it over.' He delivered her a searching glance as she sat up, pushing her copper hair off her brow, her drowsy eyes embarrassed and semi-veiled. 'I guess you do feel pretty desperate, so I can understand why you suggested it.'

Three? Claire suppressed a groan, dredged as she had been from a deep sleep. Dane was smoothing over the unpleasantness and about to unleash, she suspected, all the reasons against such a preposterous arrangement.

'For some reason, it doesn't seem to have occurred to you that I might have someone in my life who would make a marriage—discreet or otherwise—impossible.'

Her astonishment was unconcealed. 'Have you?'

A very faint bar of colour accentuated his hard

cheekbones. 'No, as it happens. That doesn't seem to surprise you,' he noted drily.

Helplessly she smiled. 'You're not the marrying kind.'

'No,' he agreed, a mocking slant to his beautiful mouth, a night's dark stubble increasing his raw sex appeal. 'I enjoy my freedom and I intend to keep it that way. Tell me about Max.'

'Is that necessary? It's private ... I mean ...' she stammered under his amused scrutiny.

'What does he do?'

'He went to agricultural college. He's twenty-five, and came up here to work with Roy Baxter as a trainee.'

'So what happened to him?'

Claire linked her hands loosely. 'Grandfather sacked him once I told him that we wanted to get married. Max is in London now and he's still out of work,' she breathed bitterly.

'And you want to bestow all your worldly goods on a guy who didn't even have the interest to take you with him?' Dane derided unfeelingly.

'That's unfair. Max knows I had no choice and he wouldn't have asked me when he had nowhere to take me,' she argued vehemently. 'For goodness' sake be practical, Dane. Max lives with his family.'

His lashes screened his eyes to a mere glimmer of midnight-blue. 'And maybe he didn't want you without the blessing of yours.'

Her breath rattled in her throat. My God, what a cruel cynic Dane was! 'That's a horrible thing to say. Max didn't even know Grandfather was a rich man,' she protested. 'He could hardly have guessed, the way we live up here!'

'Adam's wealth is widely talked about locally and he was a legend of eccentricity.' Dane viewed her furious face and sighed. 'OK, I'll make you a deal.'

Her forehead furrowed. 'A deal?'

He came down lithely on the edge of the mattress and stretched out his long legs. 'What do you propose to do after the ceremony?'

She took in his implication with a fast-beating heart. 'Move in with Max,' she confided shyly.

Dane treated her to a cold smile. 'You've certainly grown up. I'll do it, however, but on one condition.'

'What?' she prompted apprehensively.

'I control Adam's estate.' He interpreted her blank stare. 'I'm not prepared to stand by and let you gaily dispose of the money as soon as you get it. Adam clearly wanted that money to be yours, and I wouldn't agree to you making any big decisions on what you do with it too quickly,' he assserted. 'You'll surely be the first to admit that you have no experience of handling large sums of money. At least, they'll be large to you but I seriously doubt he was one quarter as wealthy as this family imagines. He couldn't have been if he mortgaged this house.'

His suggestion both off-balanced and irritated her. Somehow she had expected less chauvinism from Dane. But she trusted him implicitly. The matter seemed scarcely important when he was desirous of protecting her interests and simultaneously granting her the escape route she sought. 'You'll marry me?' she gasped in sudden delight.

He sprang up again, a rueful smile fleeting across his lips like a shadow. 'As you said, it may not be of profit to me but it's not costing me anything either. And after all these years in this God-forsaken house, I think you deserve the right to do as you wish with your future. Setting aside such highflown ideals, I can't wait to see Carter's face.'

'Oh, don't!' Gripped by discomfiture, she shuddered.

'Wise up, Claire. Carter's just being greedy, or aren't you aware that Adam set him up in that engineering firm of his? They all had their dues while the old man was alive,' he completed cynically.

That was news to her but she said nothing. She was not a
Fletcher by birth. For her to walk away with the bulk of the
inheritance would still be wrong in her own opinion.

Dane swung round on his passage to the door. 'I think
we'll head to Paris to tie the knot.'

'P . . . Paris?' she echoed.

'More discreet. Hell, have you a passport?' he asked
doubtfully.

'Yes . . . Max and I . . . well, we did hope to go on
holiday . . .' she muttered.

'Until Adam stuck a spanner in the works. What's Max
like in looks?'

She gazed at him in forgivable surprise and then smiled
reflectively. 'He's not very tall, but then neither am I. He's
got dark hair and dark eyes and a beard,' she reeled off.
'Why?'

'I was curious to see what it took for you to go to such
extreme lengths,' he flicked carelessly before he departed.

Claire sank back against the pillows, rather dizzied by
her success. Dane had agreed. Dammit, Dane had agreed!
How on earth had she managed such a feat? Doubt crept in
then, bringing her down to earth with a wallop. She hadn't
considered how Max might feel about her marrying Dane.
Earlier, she hadn't believed she had a ghost of a chance of
Dane agreeing. It had been a matter of plunging into her
one option and then coming down to face harsh facts again.
Only now it was different. Dane was ready to help her.

Good Lord, where had her wits been? Max could
conceivably be furious about such a scheme. How did Max
feel about divorce? She would be a divorcee. The minute
she arrived in London, she would go and see him, and they
would discuss it all together. Dane wouldn't lose any sleep if
she had to back down . . . but could she back down?

If she went ahead they would have a home together just
as they had always planned. In that home all the love and

warmth she had been denied here would flourish. If she didn't marry Dane, there would be no wedding, no future home. Max wouldn't take on a wife he needed to support in his current situation. No ... no! Everything in her retreated from the bleakness of such an uncertain and depressing future, and reinforced her belief that she had made the right decision for both of them. Max would understand that sometimes one just had to reach out and grab happiness in case a second chance never came.

Carter came looking for her when she was setting the breakfast table the next morning. 'You can't be marrying Dane!' he thundered from the door.

So Dane had already spoken to him. Colour feathered in her cheeks. 'I never gave you any reason to believe I would marry you,' she answered.

Grandfather must be worth a great deal more than I ever realised!' he replied nastily.

'You're a bad loser, Carter.' Dane had entered silently. He looked neither aggressive nor amused, just cool as was his wont, and the momentary belief that he had come to defend her shrivelled.

Carter flung him a furious glance. 'You think you're so damned clever, Dane! You see no reason why Claire shouldn't walk in and steal what she has no entitlement to. She's not one of us!' he blazed with uncustomary fervour, his mouth a pinched white line.

A sable brow lifted. 'At this moment I'd say that was in her favour. And she didn't walk in, Carter. Claire's been in this family over eighteen years and Adam's desire to secure her future hardly indicates that he didn't consider her family,' he quipped.

Claire wished he would stop acting as if she was helpless and gave him a rueful look before saying, 'I intend to make sure the money is divided up equally, Carter, and ...'

'I wouldn't depend on that,' Dane interrupted smoothly.

'I was doing you a favour asking you to marry me!'
Carter was in the grip of an uncontrollable rage. 'God only
knows what's in your background! I shouldn't be surprised
if you've laid a trap for Dane.'

'Dane!' Claire snapped in sudden dismay, recognising
that flare of anger in Dane's brilliant blue eyes and hastily
stepping between the two men. 'Just leave it, please. And
let's all have breakfast in peace.'

Carter slammed out of the room loudly enough to let her
know what he thought of that suggestion.

'I don't know what the hell you got in the way for!' Dane
breathed. 'That . . .'

'That was precisely why I got in the way,' she murmured
unhappily. 'There have been quite enough family divisions
created over the past twenty-four hours.'

Neither Sandra nor Carter appeared for breakfast. Dane
was deep in the newspaper when she got up to clear the
table.

'Can you be ready to leave by ten?' he drawled casually.
She spun round. 'Ten?'

'I have a fairly busy itinerary, Claire, and you can't have
that much to pack,' he replied impatiently. 'I'll phone
Coverdale and tell him what's happening. There's no point
in you staying up here any longer and we need to make
arrangements. Aside of that, you could do with a shopping
trip.'

The scornful glance which he spared her worn shirt-
waister was revealing. For the barest of seconds she hated
Dane. He pitied her. That's why he was doing this: he felt
sorry for her. Claire in her outdated, dowdy clothing with
her unemployed boyfriend and her sob story. Very kitchen-
sinky to someone like Dane with his glamorous looks and
jet-setting background. 'That won't be necessary,' she said
stiffly.

He had already moved on to something else, she realised

with his next remark. 'You are still sure Max feels the same way as he did last year?'

Infuriated, her spine notched up another quarter inch. 'Of course I am. Max writes to me every week without fail and I don't know what you're worried about, I'm not likely to cling. I'm completely capable of looking after myself.'

'Sure you are,' Dane agreed with tongue-in-cheek mockery.

Carter's recriminations had been ugly, she reflected on her way upstairs. He had had little excuse for complaint when she was merely escaping the net he had cast for her. But Carter had been taken by surprise. He could never have expected this development. She wasn't even entirely sure that she herself could accept that Dane had stepped in to save matters.

Her bedroom was drab and dismal like the house. Packing her few possessions took less than half an hour. Her jewellery box contained only three items. A signet ring she had long since outgrown, a locket with a broken chain and a bracelet—all gold and all gifts from Dane. Truth to tell, no one but Dane had ever given her the pretty feminine things that girls long for in their teens. The rest of the family had rarely bothered to acknowledge her existence. Was it any wonder he felt sorry for her? And perhaps there had been a sense of fellowship, too. She hadn't fitted at Ranbury any better than he had, but she had conformed out of necessity.

Collecting her coat from the cloakroom, she left her cases at the foot of the stairs and went to find Maisie. She ought to be in by now. Maisie listened anxiously to Claire's not very clear explanation, but her frown disappeared when she grasped that Claire was leaving with Dane. 'You'll be well looked after, then.'

Claire breathed in. 'Maisie, I'm going to marry Dane and then . . .' but she never got any further. The old lady's faded eyes were suddenly suspiciously bright and she gave her a silent, vastly informative hug. Claire couldn't bring herself to erase that delighted smile on Maisie's face by adding the truth.

'Oh dear!' Maisie dabbed apologetically at her eyes, shaking her grey head. 'He always kept an eye out for you, that young man. Even when you were little. You'll be all right with Mr Dane. I can't tell you how much happier I feel at the idea of you with a husband and a family and a home all of your own where you'll be appreciated. He's a very lucky man.'

Claire swallowed the lump in her throat. To listen to Maisie, she was a fit match for the highest in the land. 'I'll write,' she promised. 'And you're not to worry about anything, do you hear me?'

'Bless you, child. Sam and I were more worried for you,' Maisie confided, blinking back tears. 'But it's right that you should be married, so I shouldn't be acting up like this. Now, away with you.'

Claire was unaffectedly wiping her eyes when she joined Dane in the hall.

'You're very fond of each other,' Dane remarked without any hint of Carter's disapproval of such a bond.

Claire sniffed. 'Yes, and I expect she's feeling terribly hurt that she can't be at the wedding but ... well ...' Reflecting that it wasn't going to be a real wedding as such, she subsided into awkward silence and she didn't speak again until they were tucked in the luxurious rear seat of the limousine. Then she asked prosaically, 'Where will I be staying in London?'

'I'll put you up in a hotel until we get everything sorted out.'

'Oh.'

'If I took you back to my apartment you'd be slightly *de trop*,' he extended drily. 'I know you. You'd feel awkward.'

He had someone living with him, or at the very least a regular overnight guest, she translated, and nodded, trying to be as cool as he was about it. 'I'll pay you back,' she said and glanced at him. 'I mean, you do know I can't settle any bills myself?'

'I doubt if you'll break the bank,' he soothed with a lazy grin.

The car ferried them only as far as Teeside where they caught an inter-city flight to London. It was Claire's first flight and, to her amusement, Dane seemed shaken by such deprivation. They were collected at Gatwick by another car which dropped them off at the Dorchester. After lunch in a lofty-ceilinged restaurant, she trailed in Dane's wake to the reception desk, feeling murderously underdressed in her serviceable raincoat.

'A . . . suite . . .?' she whispered on the threshold as Dane tipped the porter. 'A room would have done, Dane.'

A long finger flicked her cheekbone, his unsettling eyes softened. 'Enjoy yourself, Claire. Hannah has made some appointments for you over the next couple of days. She should be over within the hour.'

'Hannah?'

'My social secretary. You'll like her. She's a nice lady, and Claire—' Dane shut the door and wandered deeper into the room '—don't worry about the money, and don't talk about paying me back,' he warned. 'You're family, and it's a treat.'

'Treats are for children,' she argued, scarlet-faced.

His eyes cooled. 'Don't make yourself a problem,' he advised. 'If I have to take you to Paris and marry you, you're not going to be dressed like an Oxfam reject. Now that's blunt. But that's the way it is.'

Claire all but cringed in front of him. The aching grittiness of tears washed her hurt eyes. He was even ashamed to be seen in public with her, used as he was to beautiful, perfectly groomed women.

Firm fingers tipped up her chin. 'Do you think I'm blaming you? Adam didn't give you enough money to feed the household, never mind spend anything on yourself. And if you don't have a clue how to make the best of yourself, that's not your fault when you had no other females around to advise you,' he stressed. 'But on the other hand, what sort of pride is it that says you have to stay this way when you don't need to any more?'

She tugged away from him, wishing the ground would open up and swallow her. She reminded herself stoically that Dane was doing her a favour he didn't have to do in marrying her. Pride goeth before a fall, she intoned to herself.

'I dare say you're used to other sorts of women.' It still slipped out.

He emitted a rueful laugh. 'Don't you want to be attractive? You could be, you know. Minus those ugly spectacles and that hideous screwed-up hairstyle, you've got definite possibilities.'

Her teeth set. 'Am I supposed to say thank you?'

'For God's sake, Claire, do you think I care what you do?' He back-tracked ungenerously as he strode back to the door. 'Send Hannah away if you like. Sit here and feel sorry for yourself. But if you're a woman you'll forget that misplaced pride of yours and realise that this is a big opportunity.'

Dear God, what an arrogant, pitiless bastard Dane could be! Her fingers twisted together and then settled on the rear of the upholstered chair where her knuckles showed white. It was not within her power to tell Dane to go to hell. Dane being Dane, he might well do just that. 'Max is quite happy with me as I am,' she retorted.

Half-way out of the door he paused, a disturbing smile on his lips. 'You might want something more than Max

once you get some confidence,' he ventured cynically
before the door flipped shut.

So Dane was no more impressed by Max than her
grandfather had been. Loyal fury filled Claire. Just because
Max didn't come from a monied background! She hadn't
bargained on the possibility of Dane's interference. But
what trouble could he cause? It was extremely foolish of her
to let his comments get under her skin. Just why had she
been so agonisingly hurt by his blunt appraisal of her
physical lack of attraction? By his standards she was bound
to be a Plain Jane, and his opinion shouldn't matter to her.
Surely she had more on her mind than her appearance?

In a few hours she would be with Max after all.
Unfortunately he wasn't on the phone, but it would be a
lovely surprise for him, she reflected with greater cheer.

Hannah proved to be a tall, lanky woman with shrewd
grey eyes. 'If you'll just collect your coat, Miss Fletcher, I'll
take you to the opticians.'

'Claire, please,' she corrected. 'Where else has Dane
planned for me to visit?'

Hannah smiled. If she was conscious of the edge in
Claire's voice she ignored it. 'It's a little late to go shopping,
but I booked you into a beauty salon. That's a tight enough
schedule before dinner.'

'Where does Dane live?' she asked as Hannah ushered
her into yet another chauffeur-driven car.

'He has several residences. In London he uses the
penthouse on top of the Visconti building. He has a country
house in Kent too, but he rarely has time to spend there.
There's a flat in Paris, one in Rome and then there's his
father's house on Long Island,' she enumerated.

'He must travel a lot,' Claire remarked limply.

Hannah laughed. 'Dane's a workaholic when he's
involved in a new project like his current one on Jamaica.
It's a shame the press are still so all-fired keen to dub him

with a playboy image. He left that life behind a long time
ago.'

His world seemed so glamorous! It also seemed unreal to
her and she was still childishly punch-drunk at stepping in
and out of limousines as if there were taxis. 'What sort of
project is he involved in?'

'Resort developments. Of course, Visconti Holdings is an
umbrella for many other companies in a variety of lines.
Dane's a strong believer in diversification.'

Sun, sea and sand and beautiful, sophisticated ladies
abounded at resorts. It figured. No backdrop fitted him
better. It was hard to picture Dane behind a desk, slogging
away at office work on a gloomy day. 'I don't know much
about Dane's life down here,' she said frankly.

'He seems very fond of you.' Hannah was sizing her up
openly. 'Not very many can claim that distinction with
Dane. He doesn't give his trust easily. Then, too many
people have tried to take him for a ride because he's such a
wealthy man. Still, nobody's succeeded in my time,' she
asserted with definable pride.

Dane fond of her? With the same casual fondness one
gave a pet dog . . . possibly. In three long years she had only
received Christmas cards from Dane and of course presents
in the form of cheques that had left her feeling rather
uncomfortable. However, he had known what her life was
like at Ranbury and she had had much more pleasure out of
a few pounds that she could spend on the small necessities
of life. Dane gave very easily. She suspected it had salved
his conscience about never even lifting the phone to ask
how she was. And why should he do that? She hadn't been a
child any more when he had stopped visiting.

The optician recommended contact lenses, and from
there Hannah swept her off to an elegant beauty salon.
'Enjoy yourself,' she urged. 'And Dane suggested I book you
in for a make-up tuition. Don't forget to pick up a full range

of their cosmetics . . . I think this is a marvellous wedding present, don't you?'

'W . . . Wedding present?' More cowed than enthusiastic, Claire dragged her wide eyes back from the unbelievably svelte beauty who appeared to be a mere receptionist.

'Shouldn't I have mentioned it? Is it a secret?' Hannah looked very apologetic. 'Dane let drop that you were getting married.'

'Yes.' Claire reddened. 'It's all a wedding present.'

Before anything more could be said, she was carried off to the wash-basins, her spectacles banished to her handbag. The maestro who embarked on her long, red-gold hair made faces of disapproval, lifting up strands here and there that she had chopped personally. In all, he generally exasperated her. 'I only want it trimmed,' she said loftily.

'I do not trim, I style,' he retaliated, and someone giggled nearby. Mortified, she shut up and watched morosely as great hunks of hair hit the floor. The make-up session was worse. Tickled and pummelled, she lay there marvelling that anyone could enjoy such an event. At the end of it all she peered myopically at the blur in the mirror and then fumbled down into her handbag for her specs to withdraw them in dismay. Someone must have put a foot on her bag. The lenses were smashed.

'Well?' the female artiste prompted.

'Marvellous,' Claire said quickly, running wary fingers through her shorn hair. At the hotel she could let herself down by sticking her nose into the mirror.

Out at reception Hannah enthused, 'My goodness, you look fabulous, Claire. Dane was right . . .'

Claire gave her full marks for that flattering stunned tone she had managed to inject into her voice and remained unimpressed. Hannah was kind. She wouldn't even have put it past Dane to instruct his secretary to say something like that.

Unfortunately it was much too late to think of calling on Max when she got back to the hotel. Sighing, she wandered into the bathroom to study her new image. The sleek, chin-length bob with the fly-away fringe gleamed with attractive coppery highlights, shaping an unusual triangular face that seemed all eyes and mouth and no longer quite hers. Wasn't it incredible what could be done with make-up? She marvelled as she stared at her beautiful face, the huge witch-green eyes flecked with gold and the new sultry cast of her generous mouth easily written off by her critical, unappreciative gaze.

Dinner was wheeled in on a fancy cart. After she had eaten she donned a floral nightgown and curled up on the sofa to watch TV. It was barely nine and she was extremely tired. Falling asleep was simply a matter of closing her aching eyes.

'Breakfast . . . lord, you look like a panda!' a familiar voice mocked and she surfaced in time for Dane to pull her up against the plumped up pillows and plant a tray on her lap.

CHAPTER THREE

HER lips parted company in a soundless gasp. She glanced down at her faded and unutterably respectable nightie and the comfortable bed she now lay in. Dane was already opening the curtains. 'Do you realise you left your key in the door last night?' he demanded. 'I came round to take you out somewhere and there it was. An open invitation to any passer-by.'

'Did you put me to bed?' she snapped in strong chagrin.

Dane drew back into her line of vision, his amused smile no longer blurred. 'Is it my fault you're a heavy sleeper? You didn't even stir. Go on, eat your breakfast. I bumped into the waitress on the threshold,' he explained. 'Hannah will be here in an hour.'

'Don't talk to me as if I'm a child,' she implored.

He studied her from the foot of the bed. 'With that mascara and shadow still smeared over you like warpaint, you don't look a day above eighteen. Why did you let them cut off so much of your hair?'

Her hand brushed the tousled strands anxiously. 'I like it. Don't you?'

He grinned at the guileless question. 'It's fine, but it makes you look very different. Maybe Max won't like it.' His vibrant eyes narrowed, an odd, questioning inflection in his final sentence. 'Have you contacted him yet?'

'No, he's not on the phone,' she replied, then hesitated, reluctant to discuss Max with so critical an audience. 'Where were you going to take me last night?'

His bright gaze was lingering on her soft mouth, an odd tension humming in the air that made her feel uncomfor-

table. He shrugged, breaking the spell and swinging back
to the door. 'I hadn't decided. Maybe I'll see you later.'

As always, he looked devastating. No matter how often
she saw him his impact assaulted her feminine senses afresh,
and yet she was at ease with the sensation. It was an old
familiar one. 'Dane?'

His argent head turned.

'Thanks,' she said.

'It's no big deal, Claire.' He sounded rather curt, as if
something had annoyed him.

She couldn't think what and was rather hurt by the
brevity of his stay. But he'd only come to check up on her.
He'd probably been relieved, too, to find her asleep last
night. Taking her out for an entire evening would have
been an enormous sacrifice. Still, she understood why he
had come up with the idea. Sometimes Dane was quite
transparent. His conscience was a little uneasy about
sticking her into a hotel alone. She would very likely have
felt a dreadful nuisance being trotted out dutifully, the way
one organised entertainment for a child. So it was silly to
suffer a twinge of disappointment over what she might
have missed.

Resolutely she thrust Dane from mind. Tonight she was
bound to see Max. Her thoughts centred on him with
something akin to relief. Why did it seem so long since the
summer before last when Max had begun work at
Ranbury? Perhaps because so much had happened since
then.

She had grown accustomed to Max's cheerful greetings
when she was out on her daily walks. Their relationship
might never have got any closer had not Max literally
cannoned into her one day coming out of a village shop.

Spluttering apologies, he had stooped to pick up the
basket she had dropped, and before he had straightened
again he had invited her out to lunch in a friendly, casual

style that had failed to ignite her usual shy discomfiture. She had found him easy to relax with. Away from family and friends he had been lonely. Frustrated by Roy Baxter's contempt for 'new-fangled ideas', he had been eager for a good listener. Her feelings had deepened the more time she spent in his company. He had freely admitted that he was keen to settle down and marry, an attitude she had considered refreshing when it seemed so many men were only interested in uncommitted relationships. Nor had he laughed or looked superior when she had finally confided that he was really her first real boyfriend.

Falling in love had been so very easy. They had seemed to match perfectly, neither of them particularly outgoing and both of them slightly shy. She had been so happy when he had proposed, but that mood hadn't lasted beyond her harrowing interview with Adam.

'Thinks he's on to a good thing, does he?' he had condemned unpleasantly. 'Well, he'll soon find his mistake.'

The next morning Max had been gone. In his first letter he had explained that he hadn't wanted to create another scene by coming up to the house before he left. Being fired must have been a most humiliating experience for him. He was not someone to cope easily with stress or hostility. She had always seen that softness in his character and didn't think it made him any less of a man, though Maisie had been disappointed in him. 'He should have taken you with him,' she had said, innocent of Adam's blackmailing tactics. Claire smiled. Max wasn't the dramatic type. He'd had nothing to take her to. Still, if he'd asked she might have felt less abandoned at the time. She felt remorseful then for the carping thought that Max had put up a poor fight for her. He wasn't a slayer of dragons as Dane was, and he'd never pretended to be.

Hannah arrived punctually and suggested they visit Harrods first. Claire kept her own counsel when they

entered the vast department store. A large, expensive
wardrobe would be of scant use to her as Max's wife and, as
she had every intention of repaying Dane, she very
carefully inspected price tags, drawing back in dismay
from much of what Hannah admired.

'But you'd look lovely in this,' Hannah persisted,
displaying a fine, crêpe de Chine dress in an elegant black,
white and jade print. 'It's the latest fashion, Claire, and you
have a lovely figure. It's a sin not to show it off at your age.'

An assistant joined the fray and Claire was persuaded. It
would do for the wedding, she told herself. In no time it
seemed that she had also agreed to a new coat, a rather
stylish jacket and a flying suit that appealed to her new
sense of what was fashionable. Hannah continued to
remind her that Dane was expecting her to renew her
entire wardrobe, and Claire selected some jeans and
sweaters, a couple of washable silk shirts as well as an array
of new underwear.

'You'll need one evening outfit,' Hannah insisted.

Claire allowed her companion to urge her into a strappy,
electric-blue sheath dress, which of course had to have shoes
and an evening purse to match. Then she firmly
pronounced herself satisfied.

'What's your wedding dress like?' Hannah pressed
cheerfully over lunch in a quiet, exclusive restaurant. 'And
dare I ask about your future husband, too?' She smiled.
'You're as secretive about him as some ladies are about their
age. I gather he's not in business. You didn't seem interested
in evening wear.'

Under Hannah's warm, inquisitive gaze, she blushed.
'It's to be a very quiet wedding because of my grandfather's
recent death,' she said hurriedly, for she hated to lie. 'And
I'll wear an ordinary dress, not a gown ... She was
fumbling to think of something bland to say about her
future husband when a slim, dark-haired man in a tailored

grey suit stopped by their table.

'You have to be Claire.' He extended a well kept hand and gave Hannah a teasing grin. 'What harm can I do, Hannah?'

'Claire, this is Monsieur le Freneau,' Hannah said reluctantly.

'You see, I met Dane in the Dorchester and, since it's hardly his normal haunt, stopped to ask what he was doing there,' he proffered. 'You can only be his cousin. Strange, Dane left me with the impression that you were an adolescent in pigtails.'

'Claire's about to be married, Monsieur le Freneau.' Hannah's tone was dry, disencouraging. 'And you are, if you'll forgive me for saying so, interrupting a private tête-à-tête.'

His smile hardened at the deliberate snub. 'And when I'm almost family too, Hannah. I was married to Dane's mother, brief though the alliance was,' he retorted silkily. 'But since I appear to be *de trop*, I won't linger. *Au revoir*, Claire. We may meet again sooner than you think.'

She barely absorbed this unlikely forecast. He could not have been more than a few years Dane's senior, and it was news to her that Eleanor had ever been married to anyone but Torio Visconti. As the raffish Frenchman moved on, there was a sharp little silence.

Hannah's mouth was pursed. 'Gilles le Freneau is one introduction that Dane wouldn't approve at all.'

So Hannah had strict instructions, did she? Concealing her amusement, Claire just smiled. 'Quite a charmer, and knows it, of course,' she passed off lightly. 'Was he really married to Eleanor?'

'He was her fourth husband.' Hannah's mouth quirked at Claire's astonishment. 'You weren't exaggerating when you said you didn't know much about Dane's life.'

'Fourth?' Claire echoed. 'Good lord ... I had no idea.

What age was Dane when his father died?'

'Seven. Torio was much older than Eleanor and she was actually quite happy with him. After his death she took Dane everywhere with her. She lived abroad most of the time. It's hardly surprising that Dane grew up far too fast.' She folded her lips as if doubting the wisdom of further confidences, and the waiter chose that moment to deliver their seafood starter.

Claire waited a minute and then said gently, 'Would you mind telling me more? Did you work for Dane's father?'

'I became Eleanor's social secretary when I was twenty-five,' Hannah related quietly. 'She was an astoundingly lovely woman but she didn't have the character to match. If I hadn't become so attached to Dane—don't ever embarrass him by telling him that—I wouldn't have stayed. Her life-style wasn't to my taste, and I'm no prude. She loved to shock people. Wild parties, drugs, anything you care to name, Dane had seen it all long before he got free of her.'

Something told Claire that Dane would have coped. But she could not hide her concern. Her own misconceptions were manifold. She had always assumed Dane's self-assurance came from having a bright, happy childhood with two adoring and proud parents.

'Did she love him? Eleanor, I mean?'

'In her own shallow fashion,' Hannah allowed. 'But she often pretended he was her younger brother. She was so terrified of getting older and losing her looks. He was raised like a miniature adult. He doesn't know what family life is.'

'I doubt if what he's seen of his mother's relatives made him feel any sense of loss,' Claire mused unhappily. Dane had been dragged up in his gilded cage. He had been made tough and self-sufficient. A pang of pain touched her for the little boy he had never been.

'I think he rather looks on you as the kid sister he never had. Why did he stop visiting Ranbury?'

'He had a terrible row with Grandfather. I haven't a clue what they fought about.' She let a smile lighten her tense mouth, liking this stern, no-nonsense woman for her affection for Dane. 'You know, I used to have the most enormous, elephant-sized crush on him.'

'He's far too good-looking for his own good,' Hannah murmured, seemingly unsurprised by the admission. 'How did he handle it?'

Claire laughed unaffectedly. 'Well, he handled it so diplomatically that until a couple of days ago, I'd convinced myself he hadn't even noticed! Still, I doubt if I embarrassed him. I was painfully shy.'

'And you grew out of him,' Hannah concluded.

Was there a small question there? She grinned. 'Starved crushes die, Hannah, and even in the midst of mine I knew I might as well have aimed at the moon!'

It was late afternoon before Hannah took her back to the hotel. Impatient to see Max, Claire took complex instructions from a helpful receptionist on how to reach the Walker home without getting herself lost. The area was something of a surprise. It was a dismal housing estate, scarred by graffiti and litter, and she quickened her steps in the rain when a crowd of cold-faced teenagers shouted obscenities at her from a nearby entry. It was getting dark when she finally stood outside the tower block where the family appeared to live.

On the way up in the jolting, noisy lift, she reflected on the culture shock Max must have suffered coming from a country background to live in such a featureless, depressing place. There was no answer at the flat on the eighth floor and she rattled the letterbox anxiously. Max had a mother and a sister. Surely someone would be in?

'Will you stop that racket?' A sharp, female voice demanded, and Claire spun, hot cheeked, to see a plump but not unpretty face poking out from behind the door to her rear. 'It's obvious there's nobody home.'

'Do you know when someone will be? Look, I wouldn't ask but I've come quite a distance and I'm leaving London again.' It was strictly the truth. 'It is important.'

The bottle-blonde looked her up and down. 'He's away for the week, visiting his family,' she said truculently. 'What's it to you? You don't look like you belong round here in your fancy clothes.'

Her unpleasantness seemed out of all proportion to the occasion. 'I'll call back,' Claire answered with a forced smile.

'Stuck-up bitch,' drifted to her ears as she retreated back to the lift, distinctly red in the face. Well, Max, didn't have very friendly neighbours. Maybe that woman had been drinking or something. She had talked as though Max was living alone. Had his family moved out? He hadn't mentioned the fact in his last letter. Shaken by her inability to speak to him before she flew out to Paris with Dane, Claire slowly breathed in. She had expected time to discuss everything with Max. Now she was faced with making that choice alone, without recourse to his feelings.

After a visit to this horrible estate she saw even more clearly how hopeless things would be without money. He wouldn't marry her to bring her here. Perhaps it was wisest that it should happen this way. Max might not like to openly encourage her to marry Dane, but deep down inside she was sure he would be grateful if she did. What other option did they have in the current unemployment crisis? It might be years before he found work and she couldn't bear the prospect of waiting years more to marry.

Deep within her own introspection, she strolled out into the cold air again. To have waited so long to see him and then arrive to find him absent was frustrating, not to mention disappointing. In the darkness, she cut across the rough, open ground in the centre of the estate, eager to return to the bus stop.

She didn't even hear her assailant. A violent shove sent her sprawling her length on the wet, muddy ground and then, while she was choking out a terror-stricken scream, a weight came down on her legs, a rough hand yanking cruelly at her hair. 'Don't make a sound,' he warned.

She felt rather than saw the cold smoothness of a blade resting against her throat and she gasped helplessly as he hauled her arms out from beneath her. 'No jewellery? Christ, you were hardly worth jumping! What's in the bag?'

Another voice sounded and in a mad fear that she was about to be raped as well as robbed, the knife no longer touching her skin, she tried to throw him off her by suddenly arching. The blow to her head made her cry out in pain and then somewhere she heard a loud shout. She was suddenly freed and while she struggled, sick and dizzy, to put her wits back in order, a torchbeam shone down on her.

A pair of hands firmly helped her up out of the mire. Claire had never been so glad to see a policeman in her life, even though all the way back to the squad car parked on the road he berated her for walking across that particular stretch of ground.

'I don't need to go to hospital,' she mumbled shakily. 'I just want to go home.'

'You'll need to make a statement at the station first, miss,' he ruled more kindly, and asked her name and where she lived.

'The Dorchester,' she stammered out.

'The Dorchester what? Sorry, I don't recognise the address. It's not local, is it?'

'The Dorchester Hotel.'

'I think she's concussed,' he stage-whispered to his driver.

Claire gazed down at her mudcaked hands and clothes and had no doubt her face was little cleaner. She had to resemble a tramp. 'I . . . I am staying there,' she insisted. 'They took my bag.'

'Lost much?' one of them asked conversationally.

She rammed down a shuddering sob. 'Everything,' she muttered, and it was true. All of Max's letters and every penny she had religiously saved over the past year had been in that bag.

At the station she was pressed into giving Dane's name as next of kin. Making a statement took very little time, for she hadn't seen their faces, but she was amazed by the number of items she recalled being in her handbag.

'Is someone collecting you, Miss Fletcher?' the young policewoman asked at the end of it all. 'You'll be taken back to your hotel if there isn't.'

While she was under the impression that she was waiting for a lift, Dane strode into the room like the wrath of God. And yet she was instantly cheered by the sight of him. He stood there for a split second, magnificent blue, blue eyes smouldering over her crumpled and filthy appearance in disbelief. A muscle jerked tight at the edge of his hardset mouth. 'God, you're not fit to be let out!' he grated, extending an imperious hand. 'You are finished with her? Good.'

'But . . . but I don't understand . . . how did you find . . .?'

'They called me.' He trailed her out of the police station as though she had been in there for committing a crime, and practically lifted her into the car. 'Were you raped?' he gritted.

She blinked dazedly.

Dane flicked the ripped shoulder of her jacket and searched her huge, darkened eyes. 'I'm asking you . . .' he began harshly.

She bent her head. 'No . . . no, I wasn't. They just took my bag,' she whispered.

Dane thrust a glass into her shaking hand. 'Drink it,' he

advised angrily. 'I could kill you! I go to all that trouble to put you into Hannah's capable hands, and what do you do? The minute her back's turned you go sneaking off to one of the toughest areas in this city and get yourself mugged!'

'I don't think I want that.' She pushed the glass blindly back at him. 'I got thumped at the back of the head,' she confided gingerly. 'I doubt if alcohol would make me feel any better.'

Dane swore venomously. 'I'll get a doctor when I get you home.'

His fury wasn't bothering her. She understood that it was a release for the anxiety he must have been under since the police contacted him, and ironically his arrival had had the most remarkably soothing effect upon her. She felt safe and secure. Max would have been highly embarrassed by the necessity of collecting her in such a state from a police station. Dane took everything in his stride.

'I don't need a doctor.'

'I'll decide that,' Dane contradicted with rough emphasis. 'You might have been badly hurt.'

Her head was pounding unmercifully and she gave way to the tears she had managed to wall back earlier. 'I'm sorry,' she sobbed.

'So you should be. When I lifted that phone and heard you'd been attacked . . .' He slowly breathed out. 'I thought you might have been sexually assaulted.'

He sighed and abruptly folded an arm round her. Claire tried to gulp back her tears. 'I'll get mud all over you.'

He pulled her against him regardless and her cheek was buried against his silk shirt-front, next to the solid, reassuring beat of his heart. Enveloped in the husky, familiar scent of him, several stray and quite inexplicable sensations assailed her. Her nipples tightened uncomfortably beneath her clothing and her hands curled inwards on themselves on a very powerful urge to cling to him. She stiffened defensively and immediately he withdrew his arm, tucking a hanky into her fingers and pushing her hair back off her forehead. 'You'll feel better once you lie down. I'm taking you back to the apartment. You don't want to be alone in a hotel tonight,' he told her. 'But first I want to know what the hell you were doing in that locality. Did you get lost? It's a ghetto, haunted by the type that hit on easy victims.'

Ruefully she pictured the likely reception she would receive if she told him that Max lived on that estate. It would give him a totally wrong impression of Max. Plenty of respectable people would be living there, but she doubted if Dane would see it that way. Cocooned as he was by wealth and biased as she already knew him to be against Max, Dane would only downgrade the man she loved further.

'Well, Claire?'

She studied the dirty smears on his once pristine handkerchief. 'I was trying to look up an old schoolfriend but I must have got the address wrong.'

'You should have asked for the car.'

'It would probably have been stripped to the chassis,' she joked bravely. 'Are you sure it isn't inconvenient for me to come home with you? Did I interrupt a business meeting or anything? Hannah said you often worked until late.'

He met her troubled gaze wryly. 'No and no, it's not inconvenient.'

The limousine eventually rolled into an underground car park and Dane helped her out. For some reason that had her eyes swimming with tears again. He was treating her like Dresden china when she had made a thorough nuisance of herself, and she was well aware he had put her into a hotel to keep her out from beneath his feet.

'You're in shock,' he drawled in the lift. 'Don't worry about it.' In the bright, artificial light he bent down and touched her throat, his dark brows drawing together. 'You've got a tiny cut there. What happened?'

She relived the cold nip of the knife against her shrinking flesh and shuddered. 'He had a knife.'

His eyes blazed down at her. 'I ought to shake you to bits, Claire. And where are your glasses? I believe vanity made you leave them off this morning but surely you wore them going out alone,' he emphasised. 'God knows, you're blind as a bat without them. It's sort of cute but ...'

Cute? Cute? Coming from a masculine specimen six foot two tall with twenty-twenty vision and in the physical peak of condition, that had to be on a level with Atlas admiring a beansprout! She even bet every one of Dane's teeth was his own and that he had never spent time with a woman who wore spectacles.

'They got broken.'

'Spares?' he enquired, walking her down a thickly carpeted corridor to stop at the carved door at the foot.

She managed a laugh. 'No!'

'Then you'll have to go back to that optician and get some new ones until the contacts are ready.'

The door was opened by a dapper little man in the white jacket of the superior manservant. 'Thompson, this is Miss Fletcher. She'll be staying a few days and, as you can see, she's had a bit of an accident, so if you could call a doctor ...' Dane's voice trailed off as he herded her past the older man's stunned visage. Suddenly chuckling, he bent down to whisper, 'I've always wanted to shock Thompson. I think I've finally managed it. He's usually so poker-faced.'

She had no time to study her surroundings. He guided her into a spacious bedroom and straight through to an en suite bathroom where he proceeded to turn on the bath taps before peeling off her jacket, his fingers reaching for the zipper on her flying suit. Hastily, Claire covered his hand. 'No ... I can manage ... thanks,' she declared.

'Why are you so shy?' Dane regarded her quite seriously. 'You've got nothing I haven't seen before.'

She looked up into calm, midnight-blue eyes and resisted the temptation to snarl back at him, for he'd been kind and perhaps he wasn't conscious of how very insulting he could sound. 'You haven't seen me.'

Disorientatingly he threw back his silvery head and laughed. 'OK, I'll leave you to conserve your mystery in peace.'

He was still laughing when he went, and for the life of her she couldn't see what was so funny. She hated the idea that he might find her so prim and inhibited that she cut a comic figure in his eyes. Sinking into the bath she forced herself to go back to that mortifying moment in Dane's arms when her body had inexplicably reacted to his masculinity. That had never ever happened to her before . . . well, perhaps that wasn't quite true. When she was sixteen Dane had had that explosive effect upon her, and she'd been shamed and embarrassed by a physical awareness she was too immature to cope with. She was even more uncomfortable with its repetition now, when Dane had simply been offering her the proverbial shoulder to cry on. Was she a little naïve about her own sexuality?

Clearly, loving Max didn't blind her to another man's attractions . . . no, that sounded even worse. It had to have been a reflex response, some sort of nasty teenage hangover from a time when she had craved Dane's arms around her. Or even more likely, the end result of over-excitement. Irritable now, she wrapped a towel round her and padded back into the bedroom where she discovered an extravagant négligé set lying across the bed.

Her fingers coiled into it with strong distaste and she raised the delicate fabric to her face. It smelt new. She put it on and got into the bed, feeling very self-conscious sheathed in pearl-grey satin and pale pink lace. Thompson appeared with a cup of tea on a silver tray and asked her if she was hungry before departing with the same silent, almost robotic air of detachment.

She guessed he was used to women here. Oversized blondes with endless legs, brunettes with the same attributes. Claire had seen two dozen over the years feature in newsprint with Dane, and they were all tall and gorgeous and glossy. Just like Dane. She just couldn't see him with anyone ordinary. The hype and the glitzy wrapping were all part of his world.

Had Dane ever been in love? Her curiosity was exasperating but inescapable. She was extremely glad there wasn't another woman in residence. She wasn't sure she could have handled that smoothly. Her brow pleated. It was absolutely none of her business what Dane did in his private life. Max had once referred to him as a womaniser. He had somehow missed out on understanding the special affection she had for Dane, and that had annoyed her. For goodness' sake, a woman could admire a man without any sexual connotation!

Claire had always appreciated Dane's strength and the fashion in which he coolly and, without ever descending to rudeness, stood up to their grandfather's loud, overbearing ways. Of course, Max had been in a different position, she allowed guiltily. One didn't hand back cheek to one's enmployer, and perhaps when he'd left Ranbury, he'd still been hoping to receive a reference. Nor would she have wanted Max to be like Dane.

They were complete opposites. Her life with Max would be peaceful and ordered and very much based on home and family, and naturally that would sound stultifying to Dane. He'd never had either, and to a free spirit, those sort of down-to-earth aspirations bore a close resemblance to a suffocating cage. Dane was the antithesis of peaceful. He raced through the day with an energy that was boundless and rather overpowering.

The doctor arrived, ushered in by Thompson. He was clearly from the private sector, and when that miserably tiny cut on her throat won her a painful anti-tetanus injection, she was relieved to see the back of his well bred head.

'I know you said you weren't hungry, but you missed dinner,' Dane said lazily, strolling in with a tray. 'I told Thompson to make you an omelette.'

'Did anyone ever ask you to knock on doors?' She tugged the duvet to her lace-covered breasts.

'No, you're the only one.' Unperturbed, he set the tray down on her lap. 'If you eat, you'll sleep better, and we're flying to Paris in forty-eight hours, so you need your rest.'

Forty-eight hours. That seemed so terrifyingly close. To conceal her sudden attack of uncertainty she blurted out the thought that had been at the back of her mind since her arrival here in his apartment. 'I had this idea you had someone living here.'

He didn't move a muscle. 'Past tense is correct.'

'Oh!' A tactful withdrawal seemed sensible. She didn't know what had possessed her to pry. 'I'm sorry.'

'Sorry?' A faintly feral smile marked his beautiful mouth.

'Was she in love with you?' She couldn't help asking the question, her belief being that Dane would always be the one to back out of any relationsip that got too heavy.

'She wasn't in love with anything beyond my cheque book and the high I could give her in bed. In that order,' he answered with smooth emphasis.

Hot colour rose in her cheeks. 'If that was all she meant to you,' she replied stiffly. 'It was just as well she did go.'

'Good sex is fun, Claire. Nothing else.' He cast her a slow, coolly enquiring appraisal. 'Next question?'

She lifted her knife and fork. 'I shouldn't have asked.'

'Well, you won't mind if I ask a personal question,' Dane assumed. 'Tell me, when am I to meet Max?'

Her fork froze half-way down to the crisp, golden omelette. 'He's out of town right now.'

'And you discovered that without visiting or phoning him?'

He was uncomfortably astute. She still carved into the omelette. 'I phoned a friend of his. Naturally I want to see him. I just can't get hold of him right at this moment,' she imparted, glad to be truthful on one count. 'One half of me says that's providential. I'm a bit worried he wouldn't approve of all this and I was wondering if you had had any second thoughts.'

'If you want to call it off just say so,' Dane responded with irritating impartiality. 'Think about it overnight.'

CHAPTER FOUR

THE dulled throb of the jet engines was giving her a faint headache. Or was it her nerves? Seemingly impervious to such sensibility, Dane was on the phone speaking in fluent French, the papers he had been studying with his legal advisor, Lew Harrison, resting on the luxurious cabin's built-in desk. Receiving a cool glance from the lawyer opposite, Claire angrily dropped her eyes back to the magazine on her lap.

She had made Lew's acquaintance early yesterday at the apartment. Dane had been out when the lawyer called with a document that required her signature. His hostility had needed no vocal utterance to be felt.

'What exactly does this mean?' she had asked apologetically.

'It gives Dane control of your future inheritance, Miss Fletcher. A purely supervisory control lasting only for the next year,' he specified, coldly concise, the bland smile on his face slipping. 'At the end of that period the money becomes yours to do with as you wish. Dane considers this arrangement necessary.'

His unveiled contempt was an unpleasant surprise. 'I take it you don't approve, Mr Harrison.'

'I don't believe I said any such thing, Miss Fletcher.'

'You don't need to say anything,' she replied as she signed. 'It's obvious you don't approve. Perhaps you'd care to tell me why.'

He returned the agreement to his case. 'I'm aware of the marriage that is to take place.' As he dropped the news, he flipped down the lid on his case and locked it. 'And I don't like it at all. Dane appears to be distracted by your financial responsibilites and he wouldn't agree to me presenting you with a pre-nuptial contract,' he imparted tonelessly.

'I wouldn't touch a penny of Dane's money, Mr Harrison,' Claire protested, horrified by the insinuation. 'The ceremony will only be a formality.'

His scrutiny showed he was unimpressed. 'A formality which will legally entitle you to claim on Visconti Holdings, Miss Fletcher. Something more than a mere formality in my terminology. Dane's worth millions. Yet because he trusts you he's taking not a single step to protect his own interests,' he informed her drily. 'Naturally I disapprove but I reserve judgement. My apologies if I have misinterpreted your intentions.'

'Of course, you prefer to be blunt,' she said shakily.

He held her furious gaze. 'It's more in the nature of a warning, Miss Fletcher. It will be me whom you come up against should the situation alter.'

His cynical conviction that she had designs on Dane's wealth had shocked Claire. That he believed she was relying heavily on the family relationship to allay any doubts Dane might otherwise have had shook her more. She had been too mortified to raise the subject openly with Dane. After all, Lew Harrison would soon see that he had nothing to worry about.

Over dinner last night she had deliberately asked Dane if Adam's estate was likely to be sorted out in the near future. The sooner she was independent of Dane's generosity, the happier she would be.

'Getting impatient?' he had probed huskily. 'I don't understand why he let his affairs get in such a mess when he knew he was dying. I would have thought he would leave everything in apple pie order. Still, maybe he just lost heart.

One could scarcely blame him in the circumstances.'

She studied him worriedly. 'What's causing the hold-up?'

'Nothing specific. Coverdale couldn't trace those South African investments. I suspect Adam was up to tax dodging, he laid so many false trails.'

'He wouldn't have done that,' she interrupted. 'He was very straight in business.'

Dane shrugged. 'Nobody as miserly as Adam could be entirely true blue, Claire. But there's no need for you to worry. I've put the problem in the hands of my own staff. Let's face it, Coverdale's out of his element.'

She had been troubled by that conversation. Her grandfather had been compulsively tidy about keeping account books. A door shut and she sank back to the present as Lew Harrison left the cabin.

'You're extraordinarily quiet. We'll be landing soon.' Dane leant back with indolent grace in his chair, and rebuttoned his shirt collar and fixed the tie he had loosened. 'Lew's cold shoulder getting to you? I did notice, but a good lawyer is not one who keeps his mouth shut when you tell him to,' he drawled. 'And I reckon you can cope with it.'

In the expensively cut navy suit, he looked incredibly cool and sophisticated and rather unfamiliar. 'Sticks and stones,' she said lightly. 'You know, I hardly recognise you in a suit.'

His smile acknowledged her less than deft change of subject. 'It is a once only occasion.'

'Some day you'll go through it for real,' she forecast.

Dane emitted a soft laugh. 'No way! That's one charade I don't plan to play a part in.'

'Ever?' she prompted, a spasm of sadness passing over her, regret that he would never let anyone get that close.

'I don't feel any overwhelming need to duplicate myself

in the next generation, either.' He surveyed her mockingly. 'Whereas I suspect you can't wait.'

She flushed. 'Why shouldn't I want a baby? I don't need to apologise for that.'

His expressive mouth quirked. 'Claire, you're a breath of fresh air.'

She tilted her chin. 'It'll be the first time in my life that I have a real sense of belonging.'

'Max just being a useful means to an end?' he taunted. 'Rather him than me. Forgive me, but I had this no doubt peculiar impression that love was much more highflown than basic reproduction.'

'Since neither desire has bitten you, you can't feel qualified to pass judgement,' she riposted, but his cool taunt had none the less plunged her into uneasy self-examination.

Certainly the thought of a family and a home loomed large in her relationship with Max. However, theirs wasn't the passionate bond that the movies and books represented love to be. Claire wasn't sure she really believed love like that existed in real life. Love to her was quiet and enduring and based on mutual goals that would bind two people into a partnership. It sounded resoundingly practical. And that was how she was in her own opinion.

At his smile she simmered. Dane had no respect for marriage, commitment or for her own sex. Bearing all that in mind, she reckoned she shouldn't be criticising. Had he felt differently, he would never have agreed to this.

The civil ceremony was to take place in an unremarkable town hall in the Paris suburbs, the key word being discretion. As they entered the building, Claire suddenly put her hand on Dane's sleeve, for Lew was several steps ahead of them. 'It's not too late if you want to change your mind,' she broached, uneasy about the way in which she was imposing on him. 'I did sort of corner you into this.'

With a blunt fingertip he pushed the attractive silver-grey glasses she wore higher on her small nose. 'No one corners me.' Smiling, he gently turned her round to let her see the small woman anxiously waiting across the foyer. 'And I think any last-minute change of plans might upset a certain person.'

'Maisie . . .' Claire whispered uncertainly and a second later her doubts were forgotten. She was much too busy accepting the old lady's hug and returning one of her own and exclaiming over the pretty bunch of flowers Maisie was proffering.

'I stayed in a lovely hotel last night, and the car came to collect me this morning again!' It was clear she was still in something of a daze to find herself in Paris. 'And to be here for the ceremony!' She squeezed Claire's hand wordlessly and swallowed.

'I think we'd better go in, Mrs Morley,' Dane interposed.

'Thank you.' Unselfconsciously Claire wiped her eyes. 'This means so much . . . even if it's not real.'

'Hell, it feels real enough to me!' Dane breathed above her head. 'Anyway, I thought you'd relax more with a friend here.'

It had been so very kind of him to arrange for Maisie to come. And how very like him it was to brush off her surprise and gratitude as if it had been something too trivial to mention.

Twenty-five minutes later it was over. They were leaving the room again when Lew cursed abruptly. 'How the hell did they find out?' he raked in a savage undertone.

A half-dozen flashbulbs burst brilliantly in the dim hallway, and there was a sea of suddenly converging bodies and hurled questions. Beside her Dane went very still, but it was Lew's angry condemnatory glance she was most shaken by. His look implied that she was somehow behind the unexpected intrusion of the noisy, shouting reporters. She didn't dare look at Dane as she was herded out, and she barely managed to say goodbye to Maisie who Lew hurriedly took in charge.

On the steps Dane hesitated, abruptly spinning her round. 'Are you responsible for this circus?' he demanded, anger shimmering rawly in his brilliant gaze.

Her eyes were still following Maisie, her hand lifted in a weak farewell to the old lady who was climbing into another car. Fortunately she hadn't realised anything was wrong. The immediacy of Dane's accusation shook her. His next action devastated what remained of her crumbling poise.

In full view of everyone his strong hands trapped her slim body to his and his mouth swooped down, brutally hard on hers, driving the breath from her in a kiss of humiliating punishment. When he freed her, her fingers crept up involuntarily to her bruised lips, her dazed, uncomprehending eyes pinned to his as she tasted the bittersweetness of blood on her tongue.

'Just get in the car.' His hand fastened to her forearm and thrust her the rest of the way.

She hunched in the corner, afraid to speak. It was slowly and agonisingly sinking in on her why he was so very angry. Those photographs had blown the secrecy of their marriage of convenience apart. The photos would be splashed all over the newspapers and the glossy magazines. It was a damage which neither words nor actions could undo. In another few hours Dane's jet-set, socialite acquaintances would be staggered to learn that Dane Visconti had married an incredibly ordinary redhead·with neither extravagant beauty nor talent to recommend her.

'It wasn't anything to do with me,' she said finally.

It was not Dane but Lew who answered, which somehow

made her feel worse. 'Someone tipped them off.'

She linked her trembling hands. 'It wasn't me! For goodness' sake, why would I do that?' she appealed.

'No one else knew,' Dane cut in.

Not a single word was exchanged on the flight back to London. Dane was seething and she pretended to fall asleep because she was so wretched in the other man's presence, certain she had him to blame for Dane's peculiarly fast change of attitude. When they reached the apartment, the strain was making her feel physically ill but at least Lew was no longer with them.

'I swear it wasn't me,' she murmured, following Dane into the split-level lounge. 'I'll swear on a Bible if you like. I told no one about the wedding. I didn't even tell Hannah. Dane?'

Ignoring her, he poured himself a shot of whisky from a decanter on one of the low oak-carved units.

Claire hovered. 'Look, I'll get out of here now,' she promised.

Dane swung round. 'To go where? Max? Move in with another guy the day you marry me?' he outlined curtly, his mouth twisting in eloquent incredulity. 'Like hell you will! As far as everyone is concerned, you're now my wife.'

She tautened. 'But we know that's not true.'

He appraised her with cold intensity. 'No, it's not but I could be forgiven for beginning to wonder.'

'We could get an annulment,' she pointed out wildly. 'Then we wouldn't be married any more.'

'An annulment?' he repeated harshly, staring at her in disbelief. 'Let you make a bigger fool of me in public?'

'I just thought . . .'

'Forget it. That's out of the question. But if I find this is a trap, Claire, you'll wish you'd stayed out of my path.'

Stockstill, she whispered, 'A trap?'

Hard blue eyes glittered before his black lashes swept down. 'Just one too many coincidences,' he breathed and strode over to the phone, punching out a number, not removing his eyes from her once. 'Any joy yet, Ken?' His strong jawline tensed. 'OK, ring me when you can stand by that,' he advised and dropped the receiver back down on to its cradle.

'Is there something wrong?' she muttered.

Something was terribly wrong, above and beyond those reporters besieging them in Paris and again in London. It was written in every aggressive line of his long, lean body, his eyes so bright a blue they were opaque. 'If I were you, I'd ask Thompson for a late lunch in your room.'

The tip of her tongue crept out to wet her dried lips. 'Dane?'

'You sound like a repeating clock, Claire, and it's very, very irritating,' he murmured. 'Do as I ask before I get less polite.'

'. . . polite?' she echoed on the brink of tears. How dared he dismiss her like a naughty child to her room! But she went because she was at a total loss and he was in a very dangerous mood, an aura of scantily leashed violence clinging to him, though he had yet to raise his voice, yet to hurt her—apart from that loathsome kiss.

'The remainder of your clothes have arrived, madam. I took the liberty of hanging them.' Thompson stepped out in front of her with the merest hint of a smile.

'Clothes?' What clothes was he talking about?

'May I ask if you wish a maid to be hired, Mrs Visconti?'

Claire froze three steps past him and surprised a grin on the older man's features. Damn him, he'd only been testing her.

'I'm very happy . . .' he announced stertorously.

'Oh no . . . please don't let Dane know you know!' Claire

hissed in despair. 'Please Thompson—it would be the last
straw . . .'

Impervious to his avid curiosity, Claire fled. She
snatched up the phone in her room and rang directory
enquiries for the number of the one friend she did have in
London. She had gone to school with Randy, who was now
a model. The line was engaged, which was more than
hopeful. Randy had her own flat and the spare room she
had mentioned on more than one occasion suddenly
sounded very tempting. She whipped out a case from the
foot of the wardrobe.

'If that is anything to do with what I suspect—' a soft
drawl sizzled from just inside the door '—nowhere is big
enough—not even London—for you to do a vanishing act
until the heat dies down. If you fondly imagine you're
going to walk out the day you marry me, you're a fool.'

She was on her knees, a rather apt position as he moved
forward, already shorn of his elegant suit. A pair of tight-
fitting, faded jeans that were fresh out of the wash and left
little to her imagination now hugged his narrow hips.

'It's better if I leave now,' she responded. 'Anyway, you
don't want me here.'

'Correct, but you're not going anywhere.' He shot her a
bitterly angry glance as he thrust the door shut. 'Such a
fragile little flower as you are, I wouldn't want to shock
Thompson with your screams. Not that he'd interfere. You
look worried, Claire. All your past and present sins rising
up before you? That call I was waiting on came,
confirmation from one of my top accountants in Pretoria.'

Claire got up off her knees clumsily. 'Pretoria?
W . . . what are you talking about?'

Dane lounged back against the dressing-table, a pred-
ator, coiled to spring for the jugular. There was anger . . .
and there was anger. Claire was only acquainted with the

blustering, red-faced rage of her grandfather. Dane's ability to remain outwardly cool in the grip of that white-hot blaze silvering his magnificent eyes, cool despite the highly tangible aura of zapping, raw tension he emanated, was far more demoralising.

'Ken is one of my accountants. He was superintending Adam's bundle of investments for me.'

'So?' The word was forced from her jerkily.

A tiny pulse was beating fast at the corner of his mouth. 'Just another nail in your coffin, Claire. And you can drop that innocent, wide-eyed look! Adam was as sly as they come. He taught you well, didn't he?'

Claire backed even though he had not moved. Wild explanations for his insane behaviour were whirling faster and faster in the paralysed limbo of her brain, nothing connecting to make sense.

'Only you didn't bargain on being around when the balloon went up, did you?' he prompted in a black velvet voice. 'I guess the next time I was going to hear from you was via some fancy divorce lawyer. Or were you planning to crawl back and grovel? Are you that obsessed with me? Did you think I'd forgive you?'

'What are you accusing me of?' The cry, edged by the shrillness of hysteria, came from the very depths of her being.

A winged ebony brow lifted. 'Do you love me? Is that what all this is about?'

Drugs . . . he was high, not himself . . . her imagination ran riot. 'L . . . love you?' she parroted, nearly tripping over the foot of the bed. 'Of course I don't love you . . . lay one finger on me, Dane and I'll scream.'

'Maybe I'll gag you.'

'Dane . . .'

'Tie you down?' He still hadn't moved a muscle. 'I ought

to congratulate you on the immense and naïve simplicity of the trap. It has to be the only time within my experience that a woman has relied not on sex and not on intelligence but on puppyish appeal. Well, I'm sorry, Claire. You don't look remotely pathetic right now,' he asserted with sibilant emphasis. 'Ring Max.'

Her lashes fluttered in bemusement. She was completely off-balanced. 'Max?'

'Yes, Max,' Dane repeated shortly. 'There's the phone. Use it.'

Hot pink feathered her cheeks. 'I told you he wasn't on the phone.'

'But his friend is. That is what you told me, blithely ignoring the fact that you never made a single call from the Dorchester and were with Hannah outside it,' he filled in with unutterable cool. 'He doesn't exist, does he?'

'Of course he exists!' she cried.

'Carter had never heard of him and if he exists, take me to him or get him over here. I'll even send a car,' Dane told her silkily. 'What? You can't manage that, either?'

She breathed in unsteadily. 'He isn't in London at present.'

Dane laughed scornfully. 'My opinion of your IQ is divebombing, Claire. I have a helicopter, a private jet, a whole fleet of cars, and yet Max is quite inaccessible? Where is he? Lost in the Amazon?'

'I don't know . . . all right, I lied to you!' she gasped. 'But he was living on that estate where I was attacked, and when I went there no one was in. I don't know when he's due home.'

Dane's mercilessly hard gaze positively shimmered. 'And this man whom you purport to love and who was ready to marry you at the drop of a hat . . . you expect me to believe that you don't know where he is, that you can't reach him by any method and that you could marry me without even discussing that with him?' he summed up derisively. 'Oh, come on, Claire, a child in the nursery could tell more credible lies than that! Max is a figment of your imagination. The ploy you used to persuade me that that ceremony today was a formality.'

Her control snapped. 'Damn you, he exists!' She went plunging over to her handbag and emptied it on the floor while Dane watched her like a hawk. 'You have to be out of your mind to think I could tell lies like that ...' She fumbled through the scattered cosmetics and then stilled, glancing back at him in horror. 'My bag was stolen. My photos of him, his letters ... they're all gone.'

'That was a *coloratura* performance. Garbo couldn't have done it better,' Dane pronounced grimly. 'And if Max did exist I'd be nailing his hide to the wall permanently, because he could only be your accomplice in this rip-off. Although Adam qualified most for that.'

'Don't you dare run down Grandfather!' she snapped, and suddenly started towards the door. 'I'm getting out of here.'

A hand as cruelly strong as an iron vice reached out and enclosed her narrow-boned wrist, literally jerking her back. Dane gripped her squarely in front of him, his jewel-bright eyes stabbing like diamond cutters into her starkly pale face. 'To go where? You're broke but for the clothes you stand up in, and I can tell you where the couple of thousand cleared off the sale of Ranbury are going,' he breathed contemptuously. 'To the old folk you were so keen to pluck violin strings for.'

'I may ... be broke,' she muttered. 'But I can go to the Social Services.'

'You've never worked and you're married. Catch twenty-two! You're my responsibility.'

'You're hurting me,' she bit out reluctantly.

'Stay put then. Tell me how it was all set up,' he invited.
'That South African venture went bankrupt over a year
ago. Adam lost every penny—and every penny of an
amount that was by no means a fortune even to begin with.'

He had no need to tell her to stay where she was. 'I don't
... nothing?' She read the paralysing truth of his
announcement in his grim features. 'Absolutely nothing?'
she almost squeaked.

'He mortgaged the house to settle his debts and keep
afloat long enough to fool everybody,' Dane supplied
pitilessly. 'Indeed, not only are you not worth a red cent,
you've actually cost me money. Carter will be down on his
knees in the local church, thanking God he was passed
over ...'

She was in shock. Nothing, not a single penny. It was like
a judgement upon her for marrying Dane to qualify for a
non-existent inheritance. And the humiliation of it all froze
her. All those clothes she had bought, she was thinking
wretchedly, all that money she owed to Dane. So it took
her, in her shattered state, several seconds to register that
Dane was adroitly flicking loose the three buttons that
stood between her and her underwear. Her immediate
retreat was over-matched by Dane's fast reflexes, and the
delicate crêpe de Chine rended with a ripping tear. 'See
what you made me do . . .' he murmured almost pleasantly.

'Dane . . . what are you doing?' Her hands made frantic
movements to hold together the parted edges of her dress.

He gazed down at her coldly. 'That's a pretty dumb
question and I know you're not precisely dumb, don't I? I
mean, I've escaped far better bets than you in the
matrimonial stakes. But you're the one who struck gold.'

'That's a matter of opinion,' she flared, relieved his hands had dropped down to her waist. 'If you'd just calm down ...'

'I'm calm. And if you want to know why,' he drawled softly, his very tone as insolent as his scathing appraisal, 'it's the only use you've got.'

Dane was punishing her on a level she couldn't compete on, hitting back with a cool sexual candour that left her tongue-tied. Awake now to the dangers of sending his temper right over the edge, she whispered, 'But you don't want me.'

He tilted his sunstreaked head back. 'I'm stuck with you and, newly married as I am, who do you suggest I invite to have an affair with me?'

His hands swept up to her shoulders and when she struggled he simply wrenched her ruthlessly out of the dress's folds, dropping it carelessly down on to the carpet. He caught her again before she could get out of reach. His fingers forced up her chin. 'Do you want this to be rape?'

'Dane, you're wrong, you're wrong about everything,' she stammered in desperation. 'I didn't know about the money. I swear I didn't! You don't want me, you never have ... so why do this? You'll only regret it.'

He straightened. 'Stop pleading,' he breathed. 'Nothing's going to get you out of this room unscathed, Claire, and on top of the last enthralling couple of hours, those tears leave me cold.'

He yanked his shirt out of the waistband of his jeans. 'What, no maidenly scream?'

Her mouth was dry, her heartbeat a crazy tattoo behind her ribs. She just couldn't believe that this arrogant beast was Dane. Dane, who had meant a lot of things to her in both past and present but who had never once shown her this darker side of his temperament, the discovery of which blitzed her into nervous paralysis, for she had not a clue how to cope with a male in this mood. All the time she was telling herself that the phone would ring or a knock would sound on the door . . . or more probably someone would shout CUT . . . and he wouldn't go ahead with any of his threats. And why wasn't there a lock on the inside of the bedroom door? That stray thought popped up amidst the turmoil, too.

'Dane.' One last attempt to reason with him, she told herself. 'I love Max, and if you touch me . . . well, Max isn't going to want me any more . . . and you know—' she was retreating again down the side of the bed '—I wouldn't be much fun.'

Unexpectedly, Dane burst out laughing. 'At this moment you're hilarious,' he contradicted, digging his thumbs into the waistband of his unzipped jeans to peel them off.

The amusement had failed to reach his eyes. There she glimpsed the enormity of what he believed her capable of. Coldly and calculatingly trapping him into marriage. Turning the tables with a vengeance on a master game player. What price now his casual fondness for her when he saw her every move as plotted and carefully executed? She had begged him to marry her. She had sworn blind she loved a man she could not even bring here. Indeed she had not a shred of evidence to produce in her own favour, and there was a wildness in Dane, a wild recklessness he kept under lock and key most of the time but which was flaring out of control like a bushfire inside him now.

'I don't want you.' She turned her back hastily on him to grab up the *peignoir* she had discarded earlier that day.

A pair of hands lightly encircled her slim shoulders. 'Don't you?' His tone was insultingly disbelieving, based on a rampant, raw confidence built up after endless far too easy conquests.

She fought free and still ended up tossed on the bed as if

she weighed no more than a feather, Dane calmly holding her down without hurting her this time. 'Well, you did ask me to marry you,' he reminded her cruelly, his derision searing hectic pink into her cheeks. Then his head swooped down to block out the mid-afternoon sunlight that fired his hair into a silvery aureole.

He didn't touch her mouth. He tasted the tears on her cheeks, the corner of her swept-down eyelids, before executing a glancing foray down over her sensitive jawbone to the flickering pulse at the base of her throat, a destination she found outlandishly vulnerable to his assault. She tried desperately to twist out from beneath him, for it seemed to her that if she lay like an inanimate doll he might take that as encouragement.

When he covered her mouth it was shatteringly intimate, his tongue parting her lips and invading her as she had never been invaded. A choked cry of protest escaped her. 'No!'

But he taught her 'yes' with pitiless purpose and, as she was a stranger to passion, that devilish and tormenting expertise worked a savagely powerful spell on her defences. His kiss consumed her and a kiss had never been like that before, branding into her bones an instinctive need for its continuance. When her hands were free, her fingers clung to the sleekly muscled strength of his shoulders and from thence into the surprisingly silky luxuriance of his hair, holding him to her, drowning in that sea of need as his urgency grew.

Abruptly Dane loosed her reddened mouth, staring down into her passion-glazed eyes. 'You're a real challenge, aren't you?' he scorned cruelly.

Her body went cold. 'Dear God, I hate you! Hate you!' she railed as she understood what he had done to her.

For an eternity it seemed she struggled, her slim body

writhing and twisting under his until the heat in her blood
was no longer enough to sustain her energy.

'Finished?' Dane meshed long fingers into her damp,
tousled hair, listening to the audible rasp of her breathing.
'And all this because what?' he questioned insidiously.
'You're afraid of enjoying yourself? Isn't that a little
bloody-minded, when you married me for this? And this—'
his palm instantly cupped the heaving swell of her breast
'—is all that is available so it's foolish to rail about what you
can't have, isn't it?'

'Damn you . . .' she gasped wrathfully, tears stinging her
molten eyes in a wild, angry surge; yet that fire continued
to build higher and higher in her under the provocative
touch of his far too knowledgeable hands.

He brushed aside the lace and silk fragility of her bra and
bent his head, finding the dark bud of her nipple with his
lips and his fingers. Sensation clawed at her in mute
defiance of her wishes, sensation that was hunger and
despair and seduction all rolled into one hateful attack on
her control. And after a while she lost the urge to struggle
that had become quite automatic for another more basic
instinct, an insane need that was beyond her restraint, had
forged its hold upon her, its path through her resistance and
the sensations then bordered on torment.

In that storm there was only Dane and a flashfire desire
that burned in her very bones until she was crying, gasping
she knew not what and he gazed down at her in masterly
and triumph when she was quite blind to such calculation,
her abandonment drawing an answering shudder from the
hard, virile length of his body. For the merest instant he
hesitated and she collided with the febrile glitter in his
beautiful eyes before he possessed her and even the pain did
not prevent that instantaneous explosion of pleasure that
shattered her into a thousand pieces.

Afterwards she burrowed under the duvet like an escaping convict, at sea with herself still, unable yet even to gather those incriminating pieces of self together again, or to forget what her photographic memory had journalled while her wits, her self-respect and her morality were on temporary vacation.

She listened to Dane in the shower. Her mind was a blank. She listened to the silence and then she waited to listen to him dress. But she missed his return to the bedroom, felt with a jerk of reaction his fingertip trace the exposed line of her backbone. 'Playing dead, Claire? Or were you hoping I'd come back to bed?'

Her body ached and she felt that ache of discomfort with a masochistic satisfaction. 'I hate you!'

'My appetite runs more to food right now. When you've trailed yourself out of the sulks, join me in the lounge,' he ordered in that same murderously cool voice, and she learnt that one could hate a voice, too.

'I'm not hungry,' she mumbled.

'Do you want me to dress you? And wear something presentable,' he added drily. 'This is threatening to turn into a wake.'

He had not baulked at taking her virginity. And should he have? The days when men retreated from innocence were long since gone. Dane. Her husband. A sound betwixt a giggle and a sob seized her taut body and she buried her hot face in the pillows. Dane whom she had trusted . . . yes, she had trusted him and she had respected him and, in a tiny corner of her subconscious, Dane had still held sway as an unrealistic hero, lacking only a white horse and a pair of pirate topboots in an immature girl's fantasy.

He wasn't her husband. She didn't feel married any more than he did. She felt violated. He had torn all her privacy from her and left her naked and vulnerable. How had it

happened? Like someone emerging from a fevered dream
she looked back miserably on the past hours. She just
couldn't begin to understand how Dane could rouse her to a
state of such abject and mindless passion. Max was the man
she loved. Max, with his all-on-the-surface personality and
old-fashioned principles. Dane was as treacherously beautiful as a glacier and, like ice, he burned. Surely her love for
Max ought to have conferred immunity upon her?

She wasn't an animal. Animals mated without emotion.
Horribly confused by what she had become in his arms, she
lay there. There was no get-out clause. Seduced was a great
word but it scarcely supplied excuse for her behaviour
when she loved Max. Her very loyalty should have made
her freeze. Instead she had wanted him, wanted him so
fiercely that in the end nothing else had mattered but the
assuagement of her desire.

She would have to tell Max. Her stomach turned over at
the humiliating, shameful prospect. She had never really
done anything wrong before. She had never been tempted
and the temptation had come just like Eve's serpent
proffering an outwardly innocent bait. And right now she
couldn't even begin to sum up what the end result would be.

She crawled out of bed, lingering to make it although she
had no doubt Thompson was well aware where they had
been. Under the shower she scrubbed herself raw, washing
away the scent and the touch of him in an orgy of bitter self-
reproach. If she could as easily wipe the memory away, how
much more simple facing him again would be and, had she
not had a hideous vision of being forcibly yanked back
should she try to leave, she would have been packing again.

On the threshold of her bedroom she froze, tucking her
towel more carefully about her. A tall redhead in a superb
sable coat spun round to view her with equal incredulity.

'My God!' the stranger evinced, moving forward. 'What

did he see in you? You're little and—' the heavily mascaraed eyes roamed over her '—skinny. Are you pregnant? Not that I think he'd be so easily caught, but one never can tell, even . . . well, especially with Dane because one never quite knows what he's thinking. He's not exactly in a bridal mood either, is he?' she mocked.

Claire was having trouble getting and keeping oxygen in her lungs after that monologue. 'Will you get out of here?'

'You can't blame me for being curious,' she replied coolly, turning on her heel. 'By the way I'm Zelda, Zelda Carlotti. I'm married to Dane's cousin, Matt.'

CHAPTER FIVE

DANE was in the lounge, and a stockily built, middle-aged male with improbably dark hair was accepting a drink from him. The Mouth, as Claire had christened Zelda, was nowhere to be seen. Probably freshening up her tongue on a kitchen knife. Dane strolled gracefully up the steps to meet her. 'You could try a smile,' he reproved softly.

'If you keep that harpie out of my hair,' she whispered, avoiding his eyes.

'I happen to like Zelda.'

'Like to like,' she hissed.

'Very vocal in company, aren't you?' he noted in a lion's purr. 'Come and meet Matt. Zelda's very friendly with a gossip columnist. That's how she found out so fast about our wedding.'

Matt chortled, his aspect that of a man who had already had a few drinks. 'And she rushed here to pull your bride to pieces. Or was it to dig out the details her friend Wilma didn't have? She's raving mad because she had to hear about it from a third party.' He laughed again. 'Say, this is good Scotch, Dane. Why don't you throw us out? It seems a gloomy location for a wedding night, but with us thrown in, it becomes gruesome.'

Dane pressed her down on a leather settee and he walked away from her again, talking about his last trip to Jamaica. Not a phrase did she absorb.

The room was starkly modern, yards of pale carpet merging into walls, a colour scheme that did not detract from the effect of sparse, expensive furniture. She clutched the sherry Dane deposited in her nerveless fingers and pretended to sip when she glanced up accidentally once and clashed with his narrowed, assessing stare.

What was he waiting for? A scene of hysterical recriminations, regardless of the company they now had? He had chosen the punishment wisely and cruelly. Having betrayed her vulnerability to him as a lover, he had destroyed her pride and, until that moment of truth, Claire had never realised just how proud she was deep down inside. How did he feel? Satisfied? Against her volition a heady blush swept her skin. She could feel his eyes on her, seeking to probe, and she willed herself not to meet his gaze. Did he feel revenged? Or, more probably, was he regretting the loss of control that had swept them both into an intimacy that went far beyond the bounds of their relationship?

He couldn't have desired her as a woman. Somehow that made it that much more agonising. That he could take her and forget her again. That he could be calm now, when she seethed inside. That he had demolished the one barrier that enabled her to meet him on an equal level.

'He's smirking!' Zelda's shrill voice carolled, the tap, tap of stilettos sounding on the open-tread steps. 'That man is down in that kitchen smirking like his horse has won the Derby and he's serving dinner now, he tells me. Why, it's barely half-six!'

'Perhaps they're looking forward to an early night,' her husband remarked drily.

'Oh, don't be vulgar, Matt!' she snapped. 'Why didn't you tell me, Dane? Why all this heavy secrecy? And why does she look like . . . well, she doesn't look happy, does she? You'd expect her to be crowing.'

Claire gave her a brittle smile. 'About what?' she inserted into the flood.

Zelda looked at her in astonishment.

'I believe I'm the one who's supposed to be crowing,'

Dane countered gently. 'And we're having dinner early because we skipped lunch, and "she" is the cat's mother. Zelda. Anything else?'

'Plenty!' Now shorn of her coat, Zelda sat down, crossing long, shapely legs. Her smiling, attractive features were marred only by the hardness of her eyes. 'Where did you meet?'

Dane was already calmly pouring her a drink. 'Yorkshire,' he said amiably. 'Claire was ten. She had plaits and a stammer in those days.'

Zelda was still staring at Claire, her eyes skimming over the elegantly simple blue dress and her fragile features. 'You never had a taste for little girls that I knew of, and what's in Yorkshire? What were you doing there?' Her brow furrowed. 'Good God, she's not one of those grasping Fletchers, is she? I never associated the name ... Claire. She's your cousin, Dane. That's practically incestuous.'

Claire's lips firmed. 'I was adopted. There's no blood tie.'

In the same moment, Thompson announced dinner and they all filed out to the dining-room.

'So you met when she was ten,' Zelda resumed at the table. 'How did you arrive at today, when I happen to know that not three days ago you...' She suddenly let out a yelp of pain.

'Cat got your tongue, honey?' Matt enquired with a benevolent beam. Claire registered that that alcoholic *bonhomie* was very deceptive, though it had come too late to deny her the knowledge that there had been another female in Dane's bed in the very recent past. A tide of fury passed through her, so strong that she quivered.

'Adam wouldn't have me in the house,' Dane drawled, his eyes coldly fixed on Zelda over the top of Claire's downbent head.

'That old miser would have put a red carpet down for you if you'd so much as shown a hint of interest. You'll have to do better than that,' Zelda challenged.

'I married her for her money?' Dane laughed. 'No, that doesn't wash either. To be brutally frank, Zelda, my marriage is none of your business.'

A chilly little silence fell. Claire, still reeling from that conscienceless laugh, caught the pain in Zelda's dark eyes, a depth of pain and anger that had only one source. She looked away, too raw herself to experience any relish in acknowledging that she had let herself be hurt by the ravings of a very jealous woman.

Dinner was a culinary triumph. Thompson alone was set on celebration and it was obvious. There was a faint, revealing quirk to his normally bland mouth. He broke out champagne and Zelda talked, talked, talked, incessantly, like a tap without a washer, contriving often to be amusing while she name-dropped and listed snob resorts and pretended surprise that Claire had never travelled.

Dane never once betrayed the tension that lay between them. She recognised that he wouldn't let anyone shoot her down even though he had no compunction about hurting her himself. It was an odd little twist in him that had always been there.

'I think it's time we left,' Zelda said rather abruptly over the coffee cups and immediately stood up. 'I left my coat in your room, Claire.'

She picked up her fur slowly. 'You don't bitch back, do you? He would like that. I suppose I ought to apologise but it was a shock to hear he'd got married. I had an affair with Dane before he introduced me to Matt,' she elucidated almost defiantly. 'I'm not envious now, because he doesn't love you. He's also constitutionally incapable of fidelity for any length of time, and I don't envy you the competition out there. I'll even give you a piece of advice for free. Don't ever crowd him. He hates that.' Raising the collar of her coat she gave Claire a cool smile. 'You see, I've saved you asking any awkward questions.'

Strain showed in her tightened mouth and Claire, rather taken aback by that depth of brazen honesty, just followed her out to the hall where Zelda's farewell to them both was a masterpiece of mocking amusement.

'How long have they been married?' The question got her up the stairs and back into a seat as distant from his tall, lean figure and her covert physical awareness of him now, as she could decently get.

'About a decade. They don't exactly improve one's view of happily ever after, do they? Still, that's their business,' Dane retorted carelessly. 'What are you planning to say to me, Claire? Where do we go from here? No place but where we are now. When I want a separation, I'll tell you. Meanwhile, you stay.'

She interlaced her cold fingers. 'I can't live like that.'

'You've already begun. I'd remind you that I didn't invite you into my life. What you find there, and whether or not it's to your taste is immaterial to me,' he drawled flatteningly. 'You were right. You're not a child but I much preferred the child you were to the woman you've become.'

His words fell on her like separate blows. A terrible hollowness seemed to be opening up inside her as she grasped his implacability. She left her seat, her hands making a sudden desperate and silent gesture. 'I didn't know. What do I have to do to convince you?'

'I'm going out for a while.' He just walked away from her, and she wondered abstractedly if there could come a time when his ability to walk away would hurt. Dear God, it already hurt. Their old ease of communication was gone. Nothing she could say would penetrate Dane's ingrained cynicism and, once he had vented his anger, it seemed that for him the slate was washed clean again. Damn him, how could he be so cool? Didn't he know what he had done?

'By the way——' he paused at the top of the steps, the

long graceful sweep of his body momentarily captured beneath the arc of a light: he was golden and untouchable and she glimpsed that cold beauty with an apprehension she could not conceal, danger signals sparking in the air like warning flares because he was so still '—I told Thompson to shift your clothes into my room. You'll sleep there from now on.'

Between the vibrant wings of her hair the pale triangle of her face froze. 'No!'

'I didn't ask a question, and if you're not there when I come home I'll put you there. A scene in the middle of the night isn't likely to leave you much dignity. One scene a day exhausts my patience.'

'You . . . bastard,' she whispered furiously.

He viewed her with hard mockery. 'Was it worth it? Was it like your fantasy or was it too real? I don't deal in illusions so don't expect me to apologise for smashing yours.'

She wanted to look on Dane as unemotionally as he looked on her. But it wasn't in her not to feel, and his lovemaking had forged ties within her that she didn't want to examine but couldn't suppress. Even though her mind told her she owed him nothing, something much more female and old as time was currently bound up in wondering where he was heading and who he might be going to and did he really need to humiliate her any further by disappearing tonight of all nights?

She relived Zelda's bitter response to Dane's marriage and shuddered. All these years and she still wasn't clear of him. She must have been crazy about Dane once and had he even known, had he even cared? His affairs never lasted very long. He bored very easily, very quickly. So how long could this marriage he couldn't quickly repudiate last? A week, two weeks? How long would it take him to admit that he was bored? But this wasn't an affair, it was an act of revenge. To keep her here when he didn't want her, when that elemental, purely physical oblivion had been nothing to him but a retaliation for the trickery he believed her capable of. If she had ever dreamt of Dane making love to her, it had not been the entire menu in one raw, indescribable sitting . . .

And the terrible irony was that he thought he had given her what she wanted. His last words had made it so humiliatingly clear that he believed she loved him. Now that he had calmed down he had selected the most obvious explanation. He knew her too well to continue to suspect that she had deceived him for financial gain. After all, she had been obsessed by him as a teenager, and so many women had fallen in love with Dane. Why should he think it odd that a female he considered repressed, naïve and introverted could still be in love with him at twenty-three? The answer was that he didn't. And if he had thought love a likely motive before he took her to bed, her response there must surely have confirmed the suspicion. She raised cool fingers to burning cheeks.

It tore her pride—what remained of it—to ribbons to understand what Dane must now be thinking. No wonder his temper had cooled! A mercenary motive he could never have forgiven, but undying love had a certain pathos, even if it hadn't eased his contempt.

It was true, she had taken a long time to get over that infatuation. But hardly surprising when she had been marooned at Ranbury, denied both a social life and an opportunity to fix her fantasies on a more available quarry. Pride and common sense had finally forced her to rationalise her own emotions and Dane hadn't known her in the past three years. He was still mixing her up with silly little Claire who used to blush like a beetroot every time he spoke to her and do stupid things like rush out of the front door to greet him whenever he arrived, pitifully innocent of her own transparency to a male of Dane's experience. No wonder he'd always been so kind to her. He must have felt incredibly sorry for her!

Thompson was bustling about her room, stripping the bed. He gave her a small smile when he saw her in the doorway. 'Will there be anything else, madam?'

Like a lamb to the slaughter she continued on down to Dane's room at the foot of the corridor. A négligé lay like a statement on the bed. She yanked open a cupboard door and stilled, a hand reaching out in surprise at the rainbow colours of female apparel that most certainly didn't belong to her. Tight-mouthed, she slammed it shut again. Well, the last occupant really had left in a hurry! It must have been some size of a cheque she took with her. The bathroom had a jacuzzi and a lot of mirrors. Her toothbrush was already installed. After switching out the lights she crept into bed.

It rolled and lurched. A water bed . . . well, what did you expect? People don't have fun on a bed of nails. Tears seeped out from beneath her lowered lashes. Damn . . . damn . . . damn, what earthly use was it to think of Max now? It was too late for regrets. Max had expected to be her first lover and somewhere deep in her muddled head she could just hear Dane saying cynically. 'Why, are you going to be his?' She closed off that thought train angrily. What was she trying to do? Ease her own laden conscience? Max was going to be so very angry and hurt, and he wasn't within reach any more. There was a vast difference between explaining about Dane in absentia when the deed was done and her present position when the newspapers had published the marriage and she now lay in Dane's bed. Her hands curled into impotent fists and the wretched bed quivered beneath her.

The only option she had was to find a job and start trying to pay back the money she owed Dane. He couldn't taunt

her if she was self-sufficient and out of his precious private
life.

'And when Thompson's gone to such trouble, too,' Dane
gibed as she pushed her plate away practically untouched.

Claire studied the rosewood table surface. He had
actually had the audacity to wake her up when he strolled
home in the early hours and . . . well, it wasn't any wonder
that even her healthy appetite was dissipated. 'I'll never
forgive you for this,' she muttered tautly. 'Do you hear me,
Dane? As long as I live, I'll never forgive you for what
you've done to me.'

He rested back in his chair, remarkably alert and vital
for someone who had had barely any sleep. 'There's an
astonishing amount of spirit beneath that prim little surface
of yours,' he murmured. 'I like it. Except when it leads you
to droop over the coffee cups on the brink of tears. When I
think of the times I've longed for a breakfast partner who
doesn't chatter incessantly . . .'

'Shut up!' Something fierce and positively primal flared
through her at his reminder of the other women who had
graced this same table.

'I didn't rape you.' He raised a satiric brow, demolishing
her with a tide of X-rated imagery. It flashed across her
mind that if he had, she could have lived with being a
martyr. It was with being an active partner that she could
not live. And that weakness shamed her too. In the space of
twenty-four hours she had made a wealth of new and
unwelcome discoveries about herself. That Dane had both
forced and witnessed those with her redoubled her
mortification. Last night he had told her he had gone for a
long drive. He had been away long enough to get to Lands
End and back! He must think she was stupid. She didn't
believe him and wouldn't have lowered herself to the

admission in case it added fuel to his egotistical conviction
that she loved him.

'I don't like the outfit,' he said softly. 'You know, when
Cinderella got her Prince, she didn't put on a pair of jeans
and turn into everybody's idea of the dewy-eyed girl next
door.'

'If she'd got you she'd probably have hanged herself!'
Claire spat.

His husky laughter filled the dining-room.

Her small face stiffened. 'I'm not going to apologise for
not meeting your standards of perfection.'

'You're going to. In the heat of yesterday I didn't get
around to showing you the new wardrobe I got for you.
Originally I planned it as a surprise,' he delivered equably.

She was dumbfounded. Her downbent head flew up as
she belatedly realised that those clothes in the bedroom
were for her. 'You bought me clothes? I don't want them!'

Cool purpose gleamed in the intense blueness of his eyes.
She made a performance out of sugaring her coffee. Unused
to rejection of any kind, that was Dane. And she didn't care
how angry she might be making him. She didn't care either
that he'd probably been with another woman last night. It
was just her disgust that was making her feel sick, her fury
that he should believe a trunkful of fancy clothes would
sweeten her humour.

'While you're living with me as my wife, Claire, you'll
dress for the part, and I like feminine clothes on a woman.'

It was the last straw. She had meant to greet him with
wooden disdain over breakfast but even a block of wood
couldn't have remained cool in the face of such downright,
shameless provocation. Thrusting her chair back, she got
up.' Then find another actress,' she suggested. 'I'm not a
very good one.'

'If that was acting last night,' Dane savoured lazily, 'I

reckon you'd win an Emmy!' As he spoke he stood and his
arms closed round her, denying her a quick exit.

'Let me go, Dane!' she gasped heatedly.

In answer he crushed her mouth under his and it started
all over again, that unbelievably strong surge of excitement
that she had already learnt to fear. His palms cupped her
cheekbones, sentencing her to stillness, his tongue delving
with inherent sensuality between her lips until her slim
body shook with the force of the sensations he could evoke
so easily. One of his hands slid down to span the curve of her
hips, tugging her closer to the hard cradle of his thighs. His
eyes were a deep, dense blue when he raised his head. 'I
want you,' he confessed roughly. 'And you're fortunate I do
want you, so why fight what appears to come naturally?'

'This is sex,' she retorted in revulsion. His grip loosened
and she side-stepped him to stalk, badly shaken, back to the
bedroom. Why, oh, why couldn't she have remained cold in
his arms, she demanded of herself? If she could prove to
Dane that she didn't want him, that would finish this whole
baiting game of his.

'And what's wrong with sex?' He was behind her when
she turned, poised with the lithe grace of the immensely
confident, his mocking gaze rousing deeper colour in her
cheeks. 'You made it sound like some sort of nasty disease.'

If he touched her, she was his. He had proved that
indisputably this morning and yet, if he touched her again,
she was convinced she would die inside. He wanted her.
Now at this very moment he wanted her and it meant
absolutely nothing. Dane was very highly sexed and she
was available and she was new, sufficiently different from
her predecessors to possess a certain novelty value. That
was all. Nobody needed to tell her that Dane treated sex as
an appetite that required fairly frequent gratification.
Their lovemaking was not associated with anything less
ephemeral in his mind. Nor was she in any way special to

him now. She was just the same as the rest.

'Claire . . .' His voice held a husky note of cajolement. 'Don't you think you're over-reacting?'

He sounded so damned reasonable and polite! It was hard to believe the same male had ruthlessly silenced her objections a few hours ago and made love to her quite exquisitely as if to set the final seal of proof upon his ability not to become emotionally involved. Now all of a sudden he was putting his arms round her again, and she went rigid with dismay. 'You can't . . . want . . .' she stammered. 'Not again . . .'

A throaty chuckle sounded above her head. His hands anchored her remorselessly to him. 'Do I apologise for that? I'm likely to be quite a trial to you, Claire. But I'm not a selfish lover. I know that physically you wouldn't find it very comfortable, so I'll wait until your pleasure can equal my own.'

With superhuman effort she pulled herself free, her fair skin burning to her hairline with chagrin. 'I despise you,' she said, and it was a lie. Of the two of them she despised herself more. Dane owed loyalty to no one else. He was merely taking what he estimated was on offer, what he felt he had already paid for in advance in Paris, while she had no decent excuse at all to supply for her own behaviour.

'You're still getting off very lightly,' he responded drily. 'And maybe by the time I'm bored, you'll be lying awake nights praying for me not to get bored because you can't stop wanting me. I'll settle money on you, compensation for one seriously damaged fantasy.'

He was flattening her again. Rolling her out and proceeding to walk on her. Her only consolation was that he had about as much hope of making her love him as she had of engendering similar emotions in him.

'Compensation for being used? What a shame it is that sex is all you can give a woman,' she heard herself bite out

bitterly in retort. 'Didn't you ever want a woman who
wanted you for yourself?'

'Like you?'

Instead of drawing his blood, she had drawn her own. 'I
happen to be in love with Max,' she assured him shakily,
but she couldn't meet his eyes now when she said it, though
she still knew it to be true. Love to her was an all
embracing, exclusive emotion centred upon one person. It
made no allowances for a fiery, renegade attraction to
someone else. And the most unbearable thing was that that
someone else should be Dane. He wasn't a stranger she
could escape, and he was much too clever to fool. He
couldn't respect her now either, when he recalled how
vehemently she had proclaimed her feelings for Max. Her
behaviour must exactly fit Dane's cynical picture of love—
or at least it would do when he realised that Max did exist.
Then, ironically, he would be even more contemptuous.

'And you're so incredibly faithful to him in mind and
body?' Long, brown fingers spun her back to face him.
'You don't love me? I don't want your love, Claire, but I'll
take everything else becasue you're mine now, bought and
paid for just like the carpet under your feet and the sheets
on the bed. And, just like them, you have a place for as long
as I want you,' he specified coolly.

'Dane, let me leave,' she begged abruptly.

'Something tells me you don't fancy a return trip to
Paris. I did plan on staying there a couple of days.'

Her breath rattled in her throat. 'I'm not going
anywhere with you.'

'I guess it doesn't matter where the bedroom is,' he
drawled insolently.

'I'll leave,' she threatened jerkily.

'No way will you leave. You don't even leave this
apartment without telling me exactly where you're going,'
Dane raked arrogantly.

'And in return I get the same right?' A shaky laugh left her throat. He looked distinctly taken aback by the idea of being answerable to anyone. 'Relax, I don't want those rights,' she whispered.

His hands settled on her rigid shoulders. 'I think you need a little breathing space for a few hours. I'll turn into the office and maybe—' he dared to murmur intimately '—when I come home later, you'll stop me in my tracks by wearing something . . .'

Scarlet-faced, she broke free of him. 'I'm not dressing up like a tart to . . .'

'Claire, I doubt if your idea of a tart and mine match.' There was an unforgivable vein of humour in the interruption. 'You know, this suffering act isn't entertaining.'

'Then I suggest you go where you can be entertained. If——' Her eyes glanced off his.

He didn't let her finish. 'You mean that?' he grated.

If you had let me explain, if there had been room within you to trust, none of this would ever have happened, she had been about to say. But how did she explain Adam's misleading will when she didn't understand it herself?

'You haven't bought me,' she replied stiffly, proudly. 'And I don't own you. You can sleep with whoever you like, Dane. It won't touch me.'

For a shocking instant, in collision with the untamed brilliance of his lapis lazuli eyes, she thought he might strike her. Then the threat passed over, his fury gone as quickly as it had come, and he cast her a glittering smile. 'I confess I'd never hoped for *carte-blanche* within marriage.'

'This isn't a marriage,' she countered fiercely. 'You don't respect me. I don't feel married and neither do you. If you did, you wouldn't be so determined to use me.'

When the front door thudded shut the tears rolled down her cheeks. Sniffing, she fumbled for her hanky. She did not

hate Dane. Not yet she didn't. This situation bore a close
resemblance to a nightmare but she was still logical enough
to see why he was so determined to humiliate her. The
simple conviction that she had smilingly tricked him into
marriage was sufficient to bring out the devil in Dane. Had
she been ravishingly beautiful and an unbearable temptation to his masculinity, she might have understood his
behaviour. Only she wasn't beautiful or witty or ...
anything ... She hiccuped into silence again after
staunchly blowing her small nose.

Did Dane really think it so simple for her to abandon her
principles and make hay while the sun shone? That was
what he was advocating. She doubted if his ego had ever
been threatened by such bitter hostility from a woman.
And it might have been amusing had not his unswerving
confidence been based on the belief that she loved him to
distraction.

She wasn't going to find even a modicum of peace until
she had straightened things out with Max. He ought to be
back at his flat now, and she prayed he hadn't seen the
papers yet. The very least she owed him was a private
explanation of her marriage. She couldn't lie to him. She
would have to tell him the truth ... whatever that was.
That she loved him but couldn't control herself when Dane
touched her? She shrank from such a scene.

In the hard daylight, the estate looked gloomy rather than
threatening. It was busy, children playing and mothers
walking with prams and laden shopping bags. Averting her
eyes from the rough ground where she had been attacked,
she hurried into the tower block towards the lift. What
explanation was she to give Max? He wouldn't be very
interested in the finer details when he realised she had been
living with Dane, sharing with another man the intimacies
they had once expected to share together.

After her first loud knock on the flat door, she heard a burst of voices within, but it was a couple of minutes before the door opened.

'Oh, it's you again!'

Claire gaped in surprise at the curvaceous blonde staring angrily out at her and for a moment she believed she had come to the wrong door. 'Max . . .' she began. 'I thought . . .'

'Well, sweetie, I'd say one of us oughtn't to be here.' She tossed her tousled blonde head. 'Max, it's for you.'

Taking in the significance of the flimsy short nightdress the older girl wore, the fact that she had so clearly just got out of bed, Claire swallowed. 'Are you Max's sister?'

The woman flung back her head and laughed uproariously. 'God, that's a good one!'

Behind her a more familiar face appeared. 'Who is it, Sue?' Max demanded irritably and then he saw her. He frowned, scrutinising her slim, rigid figure. 'Claire . . .? Lord, I wouldn't have known you!' he burst out almost accusingly. 'What are you doing here?'

Sue cast Claire a self-satisfied smile. 'I'll leave you to it, darling,' and she flounced out of sight.

'Oh, God!' Shock absorbed, Max was now tasting the full horror of her arrival unannounced upon the scene. 'I don't know what to say,' he muttered, his bleary dark eyes swerving from hers.

'Your ladyfriend said it for you.' Her voice was low-pitched and intense, a loud thrumming in her ears that left her light-headed and clouded her brain. She lifted her chin. 'I hope you'll be happy . . . you and . . . Sue. Really, you should've just written and said there was someone else,' she managed jerkily.

He looked mysteriously different, as if time had dealt imperfection to her memory of him. In her high heels she was eye to eye with him, or would have been had he had the guts to meet her scrutiny. Instead he was hanging his head,

dark colour creeping down his neck in a tide because he
didn't know what to say. Caught *in flagrante delicto*, Max of
the sterling character and steadfast promises!

'I'm entitled to freedom,' he snapped out suddenly. 'You
don't understand. It's different for a man, and we're not
married. What was I supposed to do? Wait the next twenty
years for you? Claire? Claire!'

She was already walking back to the lift, deaf to his
frantic repetition of her name. Tears marked her cheeks
but her face was icily controlled. Everything she had
dreamt of throughout the long months of Adam's illness
seemed somehow shoddy. How long had Max had his flat to
himself? Had his family ever shared it with him? He
couldn't have told her without risking his cosy set-up with
Sue being disturbed. There was a hateful irony in the fact
that Sue was the kind of sexy, brash woman Max had
always purported not to like.

How dared he try to make out that the blame was
somehow hers! Passing the buck with a vengeance. She
trembled. It hurt to misjudge someone so badly. He was
weak and she had thought him strong. He was a hypocrite
too, a liar when she had believed him innately truthful.
Possibly she had seemed an excellent matrimonial prospect
at Ranbury. Maybe Dane—and Adam Fletcher—hadn't
been so wrong. Max could have proposed with part of an
eye on the main chance. Why else had he kept on writing to
her, retaining his hold on her affections when he was
practically living with another woman down here?

Max, of all people. If it had been Dane . . . She blundered
out into the fresh air. People were never predictable. She
might have married Max. She might never have known
that he was capable of such deception. And there was Dane,
whom no sane woman would trust out of her sight. He
wouldn't have done this to her. Oh, good lord, no! Dane

would be cruelly candid when the sun went down on their relationship.

When Dane finally realised that Max existed, he'd go through the roof to learn simultaneously that Max had replaced her. She'd sooner crawl over broken glass than face Dane's derision ... worse still, his pity. Even her jobless, unremarkable boyfriend had found better fish to fry. Her savaged pride burned hotter than a furnace. No, she didn't owe such painful truth to Dane. Before he had swept her into his bed, yes. But not now.

Back at the apartment she looked at the beautiful clothes in the built-in units. Mounds of them. Leisure wear, evening wear, lingerie she blushed to look at. All the props necessary to turn an ugly duckling into an almost swan. It was a typical Dane gesture of almost offensive largesse. Easily given and in this case grudgingly and ungratefully received; but reality was beginning to creep into her thoughts now again. She had got Dane into this marriage. She owed him the outward show.

Without really thinking beyond her need to hear a friendly voice, she tried Randy's number again. Her friend answered breathlessly. 'Claire? Gosh, you're the last person I expected to hear from. There I was, reading the morning paper under the effect of the most hideous hangover ... Lord, I dropped it in my muesli! You and Dane Visconti? You might have dropped a teeny hint,' she complained. 'I know we haven't seen each other in ages, but really, Claire! I thought you were in love with some wholesome country character called Max and then I find I'm not just a chapter behind, I'm a whole book behind!'

Claire had forgotten just how hard it was to get a word in edgeways with her garrulous friend. 'I'll bring you up to date some time.'

'Where are you? You sound very clear. I imagined you'd be abroad. Are you?'

Suddenly she saw the complete impossibility of dredging out the story behind her amazing marriage. Dane had put up a front for his friends. She had no right to spill all to Randy. 'We're still in London. I just thought I'd ring and say hello.' Claire fiddled with the phone cord, stuck for light conversation. 'How's your career going? The most evidence of its vitality I receive are postcards from foreign parts,' she teased.

'I could reach down this line and strangle you!' Randy groaned. 'How dare you sound calm! You've married one of the most divine-looking and sexy men I've ever seen and you're asking about my latest assignment? Oh hell, there's the bell. I've got a date. I suppose it'll be ages before I hear from you again.'

Claire swallowed ruefully. 'No, it won't be. I'll see you soon.' And before Randy could comment in surprise, she rang off.

Dear God, if one more misinformed person told her how lucky she was to have got Dane to the altar, she'd end up in an asylum! She wandered aimlessly about the apartment and then, as the idiocy of inactivity struck her, she conceived sudden purpose, stepping briefly into the kitchen to tell Thompson she would be back in time for dinner.

CHAPTER SIX

'I REALISE you're keen to find work, Miss Fletcher.' The older woman gave her a less impersonal smile than she had been rewarded with at the two previous employment agencies. 'But without qualifications it won't be easy. Even the most junior clerical job requires some O-level grades.' She sighed meaningfully. 'Perhaps you ought to consider domestic service.'

Claire was ready to do anything but that. With a reasonable job prospect she might have talked to Dane. But not about domestic service. He would consider that an insult. When she got home, Thompson smoothly broke into the announcement that Dane would not be back for dinner. He tacked on the supposed mention of a business meeting and apologies which she estimated to be his addition rather than Dane's.

Her thoughts swerved back uncomfortably to Max. Hadn't she loved him as much as she believed, or had her disgust and contempt numbed her emotions? She was angry, bitter and humiliated but not as hurt as she felt she ought to have been. Obviously, their year apart had changed her. She was stronger and less forgiving. His betrayal seemed just like one more hard knock she had to take, and there was an undeniable relief amidst her confusion. She hadn't hurt him and no longer had to carry the guilt of betraying him.

She went to bed early though she didn't sleep. For as the evening wore on she became more and more convinced Dane was not going to appear before breakfast time. Surprisingly, she was not indifferent to the idea. In conflict, she certainly was. She couldn't bear the image of Dane making love to another woman. It was pride, she told herself, the same pride that had responded furiously to Max's infidelity. When the slam of the front door reverberated through the apartment, her tension increased instead of decreasing.

The lights snapped on, the bed rippling as Dane came down on the edge of it. He brushed her hair gently back off her cheekbone. 'Well, you could say you didn't expect me to come back tonight.'

Her lashes swept up. It infuriated her that he had not had a single doubt that she would be lying awake. 'And why should I say that?'

He took off his jacket and threw it on a nearby unit with the ingrained carelessness of someone used to someone else tidying up after him. 'Because if I go to bed with someone else while I'm married to you, that's it, *finito*,' he emphasised coldly. 'And I don't respect you, you're goddamned right I don't respect you for suggesting I do!'

She leant up on one elbow. 'Are you calling this a marriage?'

He sprang fluidly upright and started to undress. He hadn't an inhibited bone in his magnificent body. She wondered sickly just how many women had lain watching Dane doing exactly this, and she knew with painful certainty that for most of them it would have been enough to be assured of his desire.

'Are you?' she repeated daringly, to take her mind off visual enticements.

He dropped his shirt. 'Don't push me tonight, Claire. I'm not in the mood.' His bronzed profile was remote, unyielding. 'What do you want me to tell you, that I felt good about being the first?'

She rolled over to avoid his scrutiny. 'I didn't realise you'd noticed.'

He swore softly. 'I noticed when it was too late, and to be honest I didn't much care at the time.'

'You sound much more like yourself.'

'You set me up, Claire. If you get more than you bargained for before this ends, blame yourself. But I was pleased that I was your first lover. I actually enjoyed the fact,' he admitted with savage candour. 'I amazed myself. There must by something bred into the male psyche that not even environment can breed out again. Then again, if you hadn't been so wildly responsive I don't believe I'd ever have found out, because I wouldn't have forced you. I imagine that suited you, too.'

'How?'

'A consummated marriage can't be set aside.'

He disappeared into the bathroom. In his absence she boiled. His hostility could not have been greater had she put a cage round him, and she perfectly comprehended the message behind his reference to her virginity. It wouldn't make him feel suddenly tied to her. Why didn't he just jet off to one of his other residences and enjoy his freedom as if she didn't exist?

'I've decided that we'll fly out to the Caribbean tomorrow.' As he crossed back to the bed, he delivered her bemused eyes a cool smile. 'I might as well be there and it can be regarded as a working honeymoon by anyone who's interested. It would be less odd than holing up here and never going out together.'

'I didn't think you cared whether things looked odd or not, and I don't want . . .'

'I didn't ask if you did,' Dane interrupted as he slid into bed beside her, long and lean and smoothly muscled. 'Where were you today?'

Caught unprepared, she reddened. 'Looking for a job,' she muttered.

A slanting dark brow elevated as he laughed and reached

for her with hands that brooked no argument. 'My wife doesn't work. We're married. The deed is done and I'll make the best of it for the moment. No, that wasn't calculated to woo you into fast surrender, was it?' he taunted mockingly, holding her slightly above him as he stretched sensually back, midnight-blue eyes taking in her dilated pupils and luminously pink cheeks. 'The truth is I burn for you. That's why I came home. I didn't want a substitute and I never planned on taking one, either. Now why don't you match my honesty for a change?'

His tone had a mesmeric, intimate quality that jerked strings inside her, strings attached to feelings she didn't understand. Feelings that heightened her inner conflict, for she was helplessly, secretly pleased that he should desire her even if she didn't want that desire to be carried to its natural conclusion.

His fingers plucked free the tie ribbon on one bare, creamy shoulder and then shifted calmly over to its twin. 'No ... I don't feel that way!' she protested.

'I could make you beg for satisfaction. Shall I do that? Is that what it takes for an honest answer?' His smile chilled her. 'And don't dredge up Max. I've no doubt you did have a boyfriend some time in the last few years but if you'd been considering marriage, you wouldn't still have been a virgin. No one your age enters a commitment that heavy without checking they're sexually compatible. You see, we are.' As he gauged in advance her intent to free herself, a vibrantly amused smile swept the chill from his keen gaze. He swung her over so that she lay half-beneath him. 'And it doesn't have to be a fight when we're married,' he informed her teasingly, hooking his fingers into the lightly shirred lace of her nightdress, and gently baring her breasts.

'Don't do this to me ... please, Dane.' The plea was wrenched from her. 'It's tearing me apart.'

A shimmer of violet lit his measuring gaze. 'Then tell me

you want me just as badly as I want you,' he insisted hardly.

'The truth is that I hate you and I hate myself.' In silent agony she turned her coppery head away from him.

Featherlight fingers removed her nightdress and smoothed back up over the curve of her hipbone, playing over her ribcage, every breath she drew becoming one of charged anticipation. She couldn't bear it, she couldn't bear to be controlled like this by Dane. His head lowered over the pale length of her taut body and the jolt of reaction as his mouth found her arched her body upward, a whimper of sound escaping her.

He carried the caress down over the flat tightness of her belly and her clenched hands unfurled and curled again as his tormentingly expert fingers located the silken triangle of her desire. She thought later that she cried out his name in protest, because this was no gentle, gradual seduction that respected her inexperience. He racked her with hunger and her hands wove over his sweat-dampened skin in tortured circles while he slowly sank deep into her, possessing her degree by degree until her nails dug into his shoulders, her head falling back in ecstasy. Ironically it was wilder and more earth shattering than it had ever been before.

Dane ran a possessive finger across the fullness of her lower lip afterwards, while she still trembled against him. 'This is what I can give you, and don't tell me it's not enough, when I see you like this.'

She rested her cheek against the curve of his shoulder. He knew. Oh God, he knew the power he had over her, and now that he had proved that to his own satisfaction, how long would it be before he lost interest? He anchored an arm round her and the very scent of him was an aphrodisiac for her. She shivered. She wanted to drive those devils out of her but they were there to stay. She had just become another one of Dane Visconti's women.

It was so insidious, that thraldom, showing its symptoms in a variety of unobtrusive ways when she woke up in an empty bed savaged by an aching sense of loss. Did sex alone forge ties this strong? Dane was dominating her emotions to the exclusion of all else. Was that why Max's betrayal hadn't broken her up? Her brain was keyed into a surging rush of questions she couldn't answer. She wasn't flighty in her emotions. It was a long time since she had laid to rest that harrowing adolescent infatuation, but perhaps some tiny subconscious part of her had still continued to crave him. For even now Dane was here, here beside her, inside her even though the room was empty.

And did she want to stay around for the inevitable conclusion? Did she want to have Dane stroll back from an absence abroad in a few weeks' time and in that laid back, cool style of his tell her it had been good but that nothing was that good for eternity? It would happen that way. Last night she hadn't fought him. She had acquiesced. The challenge was gone, and yet she couldn't refuse to go to the Caribbean with him. After all, she was responsible for the mess they were in. She owed him the right to get them out of it in whatever fashion he saw fit.

But she owed to herself the right of self-respect. And being treated like some sort of glorified sexual toy by Dane was murdering it. Her sole consolation now was that some good had come out of their marriage. Maisie and Sam were secure and happy, in merciful ignorance of how things had turned out for her. Silent tears inched down her pale cheeks. God, she was so tired, still so desperately tired and she couldn't remember when she had last felt any different.

The tears refused to stop. No matter how hard she tried, they continued to soak the pillow, misting the room. She barely noticed Thompson's quiet entry with a tray and the muffled exclamation of concern with which he retreated.

And then Dane was there and he was the very last person she wanted to see at her most vulnerable and she just huddled under the duvet, deaf to his questions until even that awareness slipped away.

Dr Caldwell had given her a sedative which made it difficult for her to stay awake, and his calm acceptance of her distress had soothed her.

'You have been under considerable stress recently, Mrs Visconti,' he pointed out. 'You nursed a terminally ill relative for months, I believe, and barely a week ago you were violently assaulted and robbed. The human body has ways of dealing with severe stress. Yours has probably been telling you to slow up for ages, but you've been ignoring the warnings. I expect that you've been under the impression too that, since weddings are happy occasions, they're not conducive to stress.'

'It's nothing to do with my marriage,' Claire remained *compos mentis* enough to swear instantly, although nothing on God's earth could have forced her to look near Dane where he hovered by the foot of the bed, because he had to be ashamed of her for breaking down as she had.

'Of course not,' the doctor agreed smoothly, almost too smoothly. 'Well, complete rest is the only prescription that you need from me and I'm sure your husband will support me on that.'

Dane returned after the doctor's exit and stood gazing down at her. 'I won't ask you how you feel about a pseudo honeymoon trip,' he delivered with veiled eyes. 'But I think you might enjoy it as a holiday.'

'I'm sorry,' she mumbled.

Dane dropped down on a level with her. 'No, I'm the one who's sorry.' He moved a long, brown hand towards her clenched one and then stopped, perhaps recalling how she had flinched from him before the doctor's arrival. 'The moment I stopped trusting you and you started fighting me, it got destructive. I've been around long enough to steer clear of that sort of scene. It doesn't get better, it gets worse and you've already found out that you don't like what I am.'

She conceived a violent and disorientating urge to wrap her arms round him. He sounded so constrained, so unlike the Dane she knew, and he was citing himself as the sole cause of her distress, which was wrong. Her lips parted. 'Dane . . .'

'No, let me finish.' His bright blue eyes were opaque, unreadable. 'I've hurt you and it doesn't matter any more how or why we ended up getting married. I won't hurt you again,' he promised levelly.

Her anxieties dulled and fragmented, his meaning vague, she drifted off to sleep then, reassured by his calmness. It was late afternoon when she was roused from sleep to be presented with the handbag the muggers had taken from her. Shaken, she just gaped at it.

'When I got the call I went over to the station to identify it,' Dane explained. 'Someone found it and handed it in. Everything of value's missing, but I guess you'll be glad to get all those letters and photos back.'

Still drowsy, she fumbled through the muddy envelopes and the clear plastic photo wallet Dane had helpfully removed from the sealed plastic bag. Max smiled out at her from the wallet, suntanned and happy as he leant on a fence. It was like looking backwards in time and it softened her memory of him, her bitterness easing as she conceded that it had been his very existence that kept her going through Adam's slow decline. She hoped he would find happiness with Sue. Opposites did attract.

Hadn't she found that out with Dane? He had called it destructive and she assumed he was correct. There was certainly nothing comforting or secure about the terrible conflict he ignited in her when he touched her. Only then did she register the significance of the returned handbag. Dane was fixedly studying the photos on her lap. 'Good God, what size is he?'

'Five-five,' she imparted and hurriedly swept everything back into the bag. Well, what had she expected? A heartfelt apology? Max's existence had been confirmed and she wasn't about to lower herself further by adding the news that Max had replaced her with a rather blowsy blonde.

Dane's mouth was set into a hard line, his eyes cool as ice-water and just as uninformative. 'You'll be getting in touch with him again, I suppose?'

She stilled.

'How do you think he'll react?' Dane continued glibly. 'Have I wrecked everything?'

A kind of twisted fury writhed in her as she incredulously took in the import of Dane's noticeably tense enquiries. Shocked, she lowered her lashes. He was letting her know that he hoped it would be possible for her to be reunited with Max. What else could he mean? Her fragile emotional state had shocked Dane into calling a halt to their marriage, she registered. When he had promised not to hurt her again, he'd really been telling her that their marriage was over, and now her handbag had turned up to put a neat conclusion to the mess. All of a sudden, in a twinkling of an eye it was over. No doubt he was now wondering what insanity had driven him to making love to her in the first place.

'I asked a question,' he reminded her tautly.

'He'll understand,' she muttered, because it was so clearly what he wanted to hear. Anything to get him off the subject before he probed deeper. It was terribly humiliating to listen to him talk calmly about Max. As if she was a parcel to be passed back. But then bluntness was Dane's trademark. He'd never had to consider other people's feelings. Obviously what had happened between them was something he could easily set aside. That it was also a no-holds-barred repudiation of her as a woman would not occur to him. Wasn't it after all what she had demanded . . . an end to their ill-starred intimacy?

'I own a property on Dominica. I plan to turn it into a hotel when I get the time. It's a very peaceful island and we'll use it as a base. Of course, I'll be flying in and out from Jamaica.' She wanted to scream at that cruelly cool tone, scream until he displayed some genuine emotion, but then he couldn't really show his relief. Even Dane wasn't that lacking in understanding.

'We'll be out there for weeks,' he stressed. 'You need to relax and get all this out of your system.'

Brainwash me then, she nearly said. Everything that had passed between them was etched permanently into her soul. Why was it that when Dane was patently trying to mend fences, he only succeeded in hurting her more? Confused and deeply unhappy, she slept again, copping out in the only way she could from her own conflict.

'Now you can look!' He lightly dropped his hands and her eyes were seared by the brilliant sunlight and the spectacular sight of the Trafalgar Falls crashing down on to the black rocks far below. 'See, it was worth the climb.'

'Yes.' Her husky answer was abstracted. Occasionally over the past three weeks she had been tempted to pinch herself just to check that she really was here on Dominica with Dane being so attentive and incredibly even-tempered all the time. That dreadful day in London when she had felt her world was folding in round her ears seemed a lifetime ago. Here in this beautiful lush setting, it was impossible not to relax and to be conscious that Dane could be marvellously entertaining company when he wanted to be.

They had been out on many such sightseeing trips together, although Dane spent two or three days a week in Jamaica, days when Claire sat about the old whiteboarded plantation house with Hannah and sunbathed and read. The hollows in her slender frame had already filled out and her skin was a pale, healthy gold. She loved the island and the house, adored the unspoilt glory of the nature that ran rampant on Dominica and attracted more botanists than tourists to its shores.

Dane casually tipped up the brim of her sunhat to gaze down mockingly into her self-absorbed face. 'Time for a cold drink, I think. There's a restaurant not far from here.'

It was a downhill walk back to the jeep and at the foot she sniffed the still hot air appreciatively. 'Wherever you are this island smells like a greenhouse. Everything's so fresh and alive. Not at all like home.' A faint edge laced her voice and she was irritated with herself for letting reality creep in. But of course this fabulous holiday had to end.

She supposed—practically speaking—that they were already separated since they no longer shared a bed or even a room. Dane only gave her little pecks in Hannah's presence. He never touched her otherwise. She had been firmly slotted back into her former role as an honorary kid sister. Dane had had no problem in smoothly making that switch, she reflected with a frown. Their former intimacy might never have existed any place outside her imagination. It hadn't been so easy for Claire to adapt.

'Home as in Ranbury?' he drawled. 'The Hall's sold—remember? And I don't know why you're thinking about home. After all, we're off island hopping on the yacht next week.'

At the reminder she smiled. Dane hadn't thrown Max in her teeth again, so she hadn't had to tell any lies. But it had gradually sunk in on her that naturally he would hope that Max was waiting in the wings. He wouldn't want to think

he'd done irreparable damage to her life. Much as she was
enjoying herself, she had to face that Dane was being so
attentive and charming simply because he was settling
debts of conscience.

He did feel guilty. Not that he showed it now, but she had
seen enough guilt in his eyes that day she'd been ill to be
aware that that had to be influencing his treatment of her.
Still, there was no harm in her staying on here as long as
Dane seemed content. The moment he revealed a sign of
being restless or bored, then she would know that the time
had come for her to be practical and tactfully mention
going back to England again. There she would look for a
job although she did at least have some of the allowance
Dane had made her, to fall back on in case of emergency.
She would let Dane believe Max was still in the picture,
otherwise he would worry about her. In that way it would
all be terribly civilised. She would just melt back out of his
life again.

'You're very quiet.'

'Admiring the scenery,' she assured him, hurriedly
vacating the jeep before he could help her out. In her
embarrassment she caught the hardening of his jawline and
coloured miserably, knowing what he had to be thinking
and cursing her own overt physical awareness of him.

Inside the cool, shady restaurant she went straight into
the ladies' and ran cold water over her damp hands. It was
so much easier for Dane to forget. He had had so many
women in his bed. She had only had him, and for her the
memories were slower to fade. Slipping back into the
undemanding camaraderie of before their marriage was
tougher for Claire. Dane had been her first lover. She had
only to look at him to remember and simultaneously shrivel
with a mixture of anger and shame that she could still be so
sensitised to him. Dane was across the room reading a map
when she took a seat and ordered. Nearby, several youthful

female tourists were subjecting him to a flagrantly sexual appraisal. Everywhere Dane went he attracted avid female attention. In the tight-fitting white canvas jeans and electric-blue T-shirt, his luxuriant hair streaked even lighter by the hot sunlight, he was breathtaking. He had a stunning physical aura that turned heads and it exasperated her.

'Haven't you been served yet?' Dane slid fluidly down opposite, and a waitress was over with the speed of a landslide, delivering their chilled drinks. 'We ought to take a trip into the rain forest, although I don't know if roughing it would be quite your thing.'

All vibrancy and mockery, he leant back in his chair, sapphire-blue eyes fixed intently to her. 'We'd probably have to share a tent in case some nasty creepy crawly bug attacked you,' he murmured wickedly.

Her smile was strained. 'I don't think it would be quite me,' she replied quickly, certain he was trying to encourage her to laugh about what had happened between them and thus finally clear away the lingering constraint upon her side. Oh, not on his, most definitely not on his! Not if she turned cartwheels and limbo danced was Dane ever likely to look at her again as he had in London. The wonder was that he ever had.

'And if it was a choice between me and a tarantula, you'd go for the bug, right?' He laughed irrepressibly and she could have kicked him. She was blushing and she wished he'd stop staring in that penetrating fashion as if he was willing her to be all jolly hockeysticks about the recent past. Did pigs fly?

'I take it you and Max don't flirt.'

He hadn't mentioned Max in three solid weeks. Why now? Come to think of it, she was surprised he hadn't demanded to know more about him. 'I don't know how to flirt.' She just evaded the question.

'What do you think you're doing now with those big green eyes?' he challenged provocatively and then he groaned, a flicker of clear annoyance in his level gaze. 'You're terrific company, you know, but you're always putting yourself down. You've got very few irritating habits.'

It amused her that he was letting her know she had some. Automatically she grinned. 'Tell me more.'

'You never fuss about the weather or your clothes or the food or when I'm late. In fact, you never complain about anything.' A dark-winged brow climbed. 'That bugs me sometimes. You ought to be more assertive.'

'Yes, then we could argue about where we go and what we do when we get there. You'd just love that,' she teased.

A flashing smile slanted his cynical mouth. 'I'm pretty selfish, aren't I?' he agreed without remorse. 'That comes from never having had anyone else to consider. Now I've got you.'

He looked up and smiled again and her heartbeat went haywire behind her ribs. 'I suggest,' he declared mockingly, 'we head home and go down to the beach. Maybe you'd like to take a vote on that . . .'

Two hours later Claire was duly arranged on her towel under the parasol Dane had insisted on bringing down. Always self-conscious in Dane's vicinity when she was in a bikini, she lay on her stomach. All the shapely Amazonians he had ever featured with in newsprint had been bountifully blessed with curves. Her own were of the modest variety. She was reaching for her sun lotion when Dane's long fingers got in ahead of her.

'I'll do it. Lie there.' He advised lazily.

The cool, firm massage of his skilful fingers on the heated flesh of her back paralysed her. When he carelessly snapped free her bra, she trembled, her skin dampening all over as his hands roamed perilously close to the soft underside of her breasts. Her nipples tightened urgently in response, a bone-melting liquidity surging through her lower stomach in an aching, agonising flood of arousal, and suddenly she couldn't stand her own weakness any longer. She was too terrified he would guess exactly what was wrong with her. Rolling over, awkwardly clutching her bra to her breasts, she breathed, 'I'm too hot. I think I'll go in for a while.'

'I wasn't about to jump on you, Claire.' Shocked, she clashed with the cold, angry glitter of his bright eyes. As she straightened, the brilliantly colourful beach backdrop revolved dizzily round her, perspiration breaking out on her brow as she swayed in surprise.

'Are you OK?' Anger forgotten, Dane sprang upright to steady her. 'We've had a pretty busy day and I keep on forgetting you're not used to this heat yet.'

The dizziness receded again and she assumed she had got up too fast, for the heat hadn't been bothering her. The concerned note in his voice was a relief. The awkward moment had passed over. Her only consolation was that Dane obviously believed her physical aversion to him was based on nerves and embarrassment alone. He couldn't know that heated and quite shameless longings swept her whenever he got too close. He would find that information much more disturbing when he was endeavouring to make her forget that he had ever made love to her.

Restoring their relationship to an easy friendship seemed very important to him and, every time she leapt away from him, she reminded him of something he'd sooner forget— that he had ever been crazy enough to take her to bed.

It racked her with guilt that she hadn't yet managed to subdue her traitorous body, and it was mortifying to be so easily aroused by a male treating her like a sister. She would just have to try a little harder, she told herself crossly.

Before he left her at the foot of the stairs, he drawled, 'I reckon we could do with some company. I'll bring some friends back on my next trip here, OK?"

Concealing her dismay, she forced a smile. So it had
come. The sign that Dane was tired of her undiluted
company, despite all his flattering remarks. Well, it was
silly to take it personally. They were only honeymooners to
the outside world, and Dane probably couldn't have kept
the charade up so long had he not had his absences in
Jamaica to keep him going. God only knew what he was
discreetly getting up to while he was there. Well, she knew,
didn't she? Her tummy felt unpleasantly queasy. He had to
be involved with somebody by now. Sex might just be fun
to Dane but she had never imagined he didn't indulge
frequently. He wasn't the celibate type, and the way
women chased him he didn't have to be. She squashed the
resultant nasty imagery flat. It was none of her business
now.

He left for Jamaica again before dinner and he didn't
appear for four days. Claire had just climbed out of the
antiquated bath when she heard his voice in her bedroom
next door. Hastily pulling on a towelling wrap she went
through.

At the sight of her wet hair and bare feet, he smiled. 'I
thought you were resting.'

Momentarily entrapped by the sheer brilliance of his
smile, she hesitated. 'You're early,' she said uncomfortably
and, removing her eyes from him, turned away to sit down
at the dressing-table. 'Are your friends with you? You
never told me who they were.'

'No, I didn't, did I? But you didn't ask.' The sarcastic
edge quivered through her nerve-endings. It still crept out
now and again despite his admirable determination to be
consistently pleasant. 'Grant Kirby and his daughter, Mei
Ling. He's a hotelier with a stake in the Jamaican
development. She's a model, half-Chinese like his ex-wife.
Wear something partyish. She always looks stunning.'

Her cheeks flamed with colour. 'They're downstairs, then?'

'Yes.' He was suddenly behind her, removing the comb from her nerveless fingers to tug it with depressing deftness through the tangle of her wet hair. 'Why are you trembling?' he asked conversationally. 'Didn't I tell you that you were safe? Or is it just the sight of me in your bedroom that's making you so nervous?'

His eyes had strung a jewel-bright trap for her in the mirror. 'It's your imagination,' she fended, dry mouthed. Dear heaven, he was close enough to touch, even the sunwarmed, healthy scent of his lean, virile body was assailing her nostrils, and there was no refuge from the surge of hunger consuming her.

His hands rested briefly on her shoulders as he bent over her to set down the silver comb again, and she jerked as if he had prodded her with an electric probe. The atmosphere was so thick she could practically taste it. 'If you want me, Claire, you only have to tell me,' he said, so low she was barely even sure she had caught the words. And then, in that second between believing and acting, Dane broke the spell with a soft, cynical laugh. 'I shouldn't tease you, should I? I'll see you downstairs.'

Forty minutes later Claire anxiously surveyed herself. The tawny-gold gown she had chosen was gorgeous, its beauty in the gossamer fragility of the fabric that moulded to her breasts and then skimmed in fine natural pleats down to her toes, leaving her shoulders bare. If you want me, tell me. If she did, what would he do? Bitterness knotted inside her that he could joke about such a thing. But sex was casual to Dane. As casual and impermanent a pleasure as a good meal. He hadn't been able to understand why she had got so upset in London. His mocking gibe had hurt and humiliated. There was nothing funny about the situation. One glance at Mei Ling gave her the sort of sinking

sensation she would have had on quicksand. She was tall
and slender, a Cleopatra fall of ebony hair framing her
exotic features and a scrap of red silk adorning her high
breasts, and Claire recognised her instantly as last month's
Vogue cover.

'Ah, so we have a hostess!' The grey-haired man helping
himself to a drink at the bar shone her a smile. 'What's your
poison?'

'Guava juice,' she confided with a grin. 'There should be
a few bottles under the bar. I'm Claire, I'm Dane's . . .'

'We're both sophisticated people, honey,' Mei Ling
inserted languidly and, draping her flowing wraparound
skirt about her, she reclined back on a couch with a sultry,
patronising smile. 'Dane always has a lady in the picture.
Grant, make mine a rum punch. My head's still not
together after that nasty, bumpy little plane we flew in on.
God, when will they build a jet-strip here?'

'You've been to Dominica before?' Claire walked across
to clasp the glass that Grant was extending, dismayed that
Dane had not even told these friends of his that she was his
wife.

'Once before.'

Instead of handing her the drink, the older man planted
an arm round her, his hand wandering down over the
curve of her hip. 'Say, you're kind of cute for Dane's tastes.'
He gave her a playful slap on the *derrière*.

'Handling my wife knocks you right off my visiting list,'
Dane drawled as he joined them.

'Your wife?' Mei Ling echoed, thunderstruck. 'When did
you get married?'

A little flushed, Claire clutched the drink Dane had
retrieved for her. 'A month ago.'

The model eyed her up and down intently as if seeking a
hidden vein of uranium that might clarify the mystery.

'Must have been when we were in Argentina, honey.'

Grant strolled forward, his heavy face faintly mottled with colour. 'It must've been sudden, too.'

'Not really. Claire's known me for years.'

Mei Ling tinkled with laughter. 'Oh, do tell all!' she encouraged in a throaty purr.

'Dane and I do have business to discuss,' Grant interceded. 'Why don't you girls talk about your clothes and your latest social triumphs, and let us get on with talking boring shop?'

His daughter pouted and swung her feet down off the couch, clearly expecting Claire to join her. The time before dinner vanished on a tide of desultory and trivial chatter because it was glaringly obvious Mei Ling had not the smallest interest in anyone beyond Dane, her slanted dark eyes following his every movement round the room.

'I'm surprised you let him wander about Jamaica alone,' she hazarded on the way into dinner. 'But Dane would do just what he wanted to do, wouldn't he?' she concluded with great condescension.

'Would he?' Claire opened limpid eyes, an extraordinarily strong urge to scratch winging through her.

Mei Ling just ignored her. 'He's the best looking male I've ever seen, and he's just loaded with sex appeal,' she commented with rich appreciation.

'Speaking personally, of course, I always preferred his IQ.'

Mei Ling drew incredulous eyes back to her.

Determinedly Claire smiled. 'His looks are just the icing on the cake.'

The most horrible suspicion was blossoming within her now. Was Mei Ling Dane's current bed-partner? The girl seemed so incredibly confident, despite Claire's presence. Why should Dane feel obligated to remain celibate when they both knew their marriage was just a piece of paper? His bedroom was in the other wing of the house and yes, in

Claire's opinion, he was perfectly capable of carrying off such a *ménage à trois*. The suspicion shook her to the very depths. Dane had invited the Kirbys here to stay and then to join them on the yacht. Was Dane quietly letting her know that he wasn't waiting indefinitely to take up his usual way of life?

'Knock down a few walls here and there, and it's going to be one fabulous place,' Grant was saying enthusiastically over the creole lobster. 'Then when you clear some of those trees off the acreage you own and put in pools, maybe a couples-only complex above the beach . . . what do you think?'

'Ghastly!' The admission leapt off Claire's tongue and she bit her lip. 'Oh, not your ideas, Grant, but this is such a lovely old house. I'm sentimental. I hate to think of it becoming a hotel and losing its character. Jacuzzis in the en suites and all that.'

Dane lifted a sable brow at her sudden loquacity. 'I was planning on retaining the character. This place is a potential goldmine.'

'You don't need it,' she said helplessly.

'Meaning?' he persisted calmly.

Grant was shaking his head ruefully, man-to-man-over-little-woman's-idiocy fashion. 'You're not into business, are you?'

'Sorry. I shouldn't have interrupted.' Recollecting her exact position in Dane's life, she didn't know what had got into her to speak her mind suddenly on what was frankly none of her business.

Grant was bent on re-educating her. 'It will cost a mint to put this place in order. Stands to reason it has to be a paying proposition. You could always hang on to a private suite here for your own use,' he pointed out. 'Though why you should want to before this island develops some nightspots,

I don't know. There isn't a top hotel here yet. It's crying out for development.'

Claire nodded peaceably, feeling Dane's penetrating gaze resting on her profile and wishing she had kept quiet. Money, money, money. His world revolved on multi-million dollar deals and this house was just another moneyspinner to him.

After dinner Mei Ling hugged Dane's side and hung on his every word in the most sickeningly sycophantic style. Grant expounded at length on his vision of Dominica in another decade. It was depressing. When Claire looked up she registered that Dane and Mei Ling had stepped out on to the terrace where they were no longer within view. Obeying an impulse of stark fear, she said, 'Excuse me, Grant. It's getting cool. I'll just go and get a shawl.'

She went out through the dining-room where the table was being cleared. Her stiletto heels clicked on the wooden floor of the terrace and stirred the couple in the shadows. Inside again, she leant back up against the wall, a trickle of sweat running down between her breasts, a punched-in-the-stomach sensation bowing her head. The agony of sick jealousy was a canker clawing at her.

Kissing her right where he could be seen! Bastard! Her stomach somersaulted and heaved. As if someone had ripped a veil from her eyes she saw inside her own anguish. When had it happened? When had she fallen in love with Dane? Or had it always been there, merely lying dormant because she had never dreamt that Dane could ever be more than a fantasy to her? Still in shock, she forced herself off the wall, away from the servants' curious dark eyes and upstairs to collect a shawl. Had she been seen? It could easily have been one of the servants.

Perhaps pride hadn't let her admit even to herself how completely she had become a victim of Dane's powerful attraction. Once, she had congratulated herself on her immunity. In retrospect she couldn't begin to excuse her own wilful blindness. Of course she couldn't bear other women to look at him, another woman to touch him. Of course she had treasured and revelled in every moment of his exclusive company. She loved him, she loved him as she had never loved Max.

Something inside her had died when she saw them, mercifully numbing her because she couldn't stand that amount of pain all at once. But there was nothing deathlike about the agonising bite of bitter jealousy that now brought her closer to screaming point.

And Dane didn't want her love. She was sure of that. He had never intended this sojourn abroad to be anything more than a convalescent holiday.

She had been drifting along in a sort of fool's paradise, convincing herself that she only wanted his friendship. She couldn't drift any longer. At any time she might betray herself and she couldn't take that risk. Dane would pity her. He would find another guilt trip to carry and all along she'd seen that remorse in him and obstinately shut her eyes to the evidence. The gifts, the unasked-for and unexpected attention... Dane's way of saying sorry, and that was all he had to give her. The give-poor-Claire-a-good-time syndrome, the treat for the deprived child ... it was so humiliating, and yet she had let him do it because subconsciously she hadn't been able to face the time when they would have to part.

But she couldn't let it continue. It was already clear that Dane was pining for more exciting company ... and resenting the lonely nights he spent here on Dominica. Now was the time for her to talk cheerfully of leaving, for there was no future for her with Dane. The first move would have to come from her and it would have to be soon, very soon. With Mei Ling already on the scene, her own graceful bowing out was imperative.

She returned to Grant trailing a shawl. At the bar she fixed herself a rum cocktail and drank, still seeing Mei Ling welded to Dane, two bodies in perfect sychronisation. 'Would you like a refill?' she asked Grant steadily.

'Don't mind if I do.' He was too self-absorbed to notice the twin spots of feverish colour over her cheekbones.

When the players strolled back in, she had recovered sufficiently to talk again, a haze of defiant, bone-deep pride pushing her into stubbornly bright smiles while she held her head high.

Had he yet or hadn't he? She was preoccupied with masochistic and obsessive thoughts on whether Dane was at the outset or in the middle of his affair with the beautiful model. How uncool of him to be making love out on the terrace as if some great intrigue was afoot when really there was no intrigue at all. They had never had a marriage. He didn't owe her loyalty. He had told her in so many ways of his indifference to her as a woman. It wrenched her with literally physical pain to accept the end of the evening when it came and calmly head upstairs for bed.

CHAPTER SEVEN

WHAT time it was when she finally gave up the ghost of sleep Claire had no idea. The old house was silent as the grave. Shedding her damp nightdress, she tugged on a silky beach skirt and stuffed her feet into mules. A cotton knit sweater completed the outfit. She left the house by the terrace, heading down the slope to the path that twisted through the trees to the beach. The night air was still warm and balmy, and she crouched down on the sand where the surf whispered almost to her toes.

Dane was with Mei Ling. Of course he was. Normally he called in to say goodnight and tonight he hadn't bothered. She bowed her head.

'I saw you crossing the lawn from my room.' Oblivious to the fact that his stealthy approach had frightened the life out of her, Dane dropped down beside her, his thigh muscles straining against the worn fabric of a pair of disreputable jeans. 'What are you thinking about?'

Her breath rattled in her throat. 'Going home,' she said abruptly.

'That's weeks away. Don't tell me you're homesick.'

She started to rise but his hand on her wrist prevented her. 'I suppose I am a bit,' she lied, for the last trappings of her life in Yorkshire had fallen away. Looking back, she saw lost and wasted years when she might have been out in the world finding the self Dane had somehow found for her. Tell me if you want me. The temptation to do so was incredibly strong when she glanced at his hard, handsome profile and appreciated that she had few such occasions left to her. For with Mei Ling around, she was decidedly superfluous.

'You've changed.' He threaded a casual hand through her tumbled hair and pushed the vibrant strands back behind her ear. 'I used to be able to read you like a book.'

She went rigid. 'Really?'

'Not any more. You haven't forgiven me, have you?' he murmured, holding her eyes with cool challenge, a half-smile shadowing his chiselled mouth. 'If I hadn't been so furious I would have realised that you just weren't capable of that size of a deception. Money's not that important to you.'

'It was a misunderstanding.'

'A farce,' he contradicted coolly.

'What changed your mind? You thought I was lying,' she reminded him ruefully.

'It started changing the day your bag was turned in. Once I realised Max was fact, my suspicions started to seem quite ridiculous. You were as taken aback as I was when the Press appeared on our wedding day. I'd still like to get my hands on whoever's responsible for that,' he grated.

Claire sighed. 'I thought it might be Sandra or Carter. I dare say we'll never know. Carter, I think really,' she reflected. 'He's the spiteful one. Still, it hardly matters now.'

'It mattered one hell of a lot at the time,' he argued grimly. 'Have you been in touch with Max? You never mention him.'

And that was worrying him now? Did he really think she could breeze back to another man after living with him? Let him think that she still loved Max. It was what he wanted to think. Indeed, considering how she felt about him, she supposed she was very fortunate that he did think that. She could still look him in the face as long as he believed her impervious to his attractions. That charismatic charm he could unleash at a moment's notice was basically meaningless. He had used it on her quite unashamedly throughout her stay here to ensure that she relaxed. Or maybe he wasn't even aware that he did it.

'I wrote before we left London.' She gave the lie stiffly. It was suitably fuzzy.

He cast her a derisive glance. 'Very proper. Perhaps you'd like to see this. The last piece of the puzzle.' He laid an envelope on her lap. 'Carter sent it to me in Jamaica. Coverdale had it in his keeping to be delivered as soon as the estate was settled. It confirmed what I'd already worked out for myself.'

She stilled. 'It's from . . .?'

'Yes, Adam's last words, calculated to have driven Carter up the wall, had he done what was expected of him,' Dane completed drily.

Her grandfather's spidery scrawl was hard to decipher. The gist of his message was one of sanctimonious superiority and her lips compressed bloodlessly as she read.

'His precious family milked him of his money over the past thirty years. They borrowed constantly off him. He got very bitter about their greed when his remaining investment failed to prosper,' Dane explained. 'And in an uncharacteristic spurt of daring he plunged what was left into a silver mine in the Transvaal and lost every penny.'

Her eyes were damp. 'It's sad when he was always so careful. What does he mean . . . "Dane was right"?' She squinted suddenly at the foot of the page and hastily went on to the next. 'He's talking about me and that row you had with him . . . Good lord, how could it have involved me?'

Dane searched her bemused features wryly. 'Why not? No one else up there gave a damn about you being used when it took the heat off them,' he derided. 'He took you out of school and shut you up to rot with him in that house as a bloody servant. He'd never have treated you that way if you'd been born a Fletcher. He was too much of a snob.'

'But what did you argue about?' she persisted.

'I found out he wasn't planning to leave you anything in his will. Despite everything you'd done for him, he was still acting as if you weren't family.'

Restively she sprang up. 'He gave me a home.'

'Big deal!' Dane followed her more gracefully and walked down the beach with her. 'I suggested he let me take you down to London and get you fixed up with some sort of job. He blew a fuse and accused me of having sexual designs on you. Hell, I was so disgusted I just walked out. I decided I'd extend the hand of help if you needed it when he was gone.'

Her skin was hot as a furnace. She was sick and tired of being an object of pity to Dane. It seemed she had never been anything else. From childhood to adulthood. At least he hadn't made love to her out of pity, too.

'That was kind of you,' she allowed curtly.

'Well, just how were you going to live when he died?' Dane demanded. 'You were turning into a real hidebound old maid. Still, I must have planted some seed of guilt in him that day. He did change his will in your favour. Then when he lost his money he decided Carter would be very well served if he still married you under the belief that you would be an heiress. If you had taken Carter it would have been months, not days, before Coverdale discovered that there was no inheritance to hand over.'

She was bitterly hurt by the adage of old maid flung so casually, and by the creeping suspicion that Dane's apparent liking for her over the years had been purely based on compassion for someone in a less fortunate position than himself, someone without the freedom of

choice that counted so very highly in Dane's view of life. So
he had arrogantly come to the funeral prepared to play
Santa Claus and Pygmalion! Just for once he had bitten off
more than he could chew.

'Can you imagine the life I would have led with Carter
once he learnt that there wasn't going to be any money?'
she muttered sickly.

Dane retrieved the letter from her clenched hand and
dug it into the rear pocket of his jeans. 'I don't know. He
might have been kinder than I was,' he mused harshly,
reinforcing her conviction that his every gesture since had
been guilt-orientated. 'Forget it now, Claire. It's over.'

No, for her at least it was far from over. Tragically, she
had married Dane. Dane had been the one to suffer from
Adam's manipulations, and that letter had come too late to
save her and Dane from the shockwaves.

'I ought to go back to bed.' Her eyes lingered on him,
then swerved away. 'I thought you were with Mei Ling.'

'Would it have bothered you if I had been?' he countered
cynically.

'Yes!' Angered, she stood her ground. 'I don't have to be
jealous to find promiscuity offensive,' she flared.

He caught her to him with powerful hands. 'Is that a dog-
in-the-manger attitude, or something more?' Hard
amusement brimmed in his bright chilling gaze.

'It's a very awkward situation.'

'Awkward?' Her control appeared to antagonise him.
Then he laughed softly and took her tender mouth fiercely,
and she went under as if she was drowning, trading him kiss
for kiss, guided only by raw hunger. His hand thrust up her
jersey and closed over the pointed swell of her breast and
she gasped, her knees threatening to buckle under her as
her body surged wantonly against the lean, masculine lure
of his.

He pushed her away suddenly and she fell off balance, down on to the grey, volcanic sand, sobbing for breath. Her love for him was struggling for utterance and she wrestled with it in the aftermath of his rejection, flinching from an outside image of herself confessing her thraldom on her knees at his feet. Did she want his pity again?

'I can get sex anywhere,' Dane slated roughly, cruelly. 'I don't need it from you, Claire.'

He swung away and strode up the beach. He left her there in a state between rage and anguish. She almost shouted after him. But she saw the futility of fight. He didn't want her. He had never really wanted her. That they had briefly burned together in a conflagration of desire was one of life's more inexplicable mysteries. Dane would not use her again. Damn you, Dane, for being a gentleman too late! Her clenched fist punched into the sand in an agony of despair, for she would have taken anything he would have given her now as a last memory, a last resort when pride was sunk beneath a tide of apprehension of what life would be like without him.

In the morning she was dull-eyed when she went down for breakfast, and Dane was alone at the table. 'Grant and Mei Ling won't surface for hours yet,' he forecast. 'They only flew back from South America yesterday. I'm sorry about last night.'

She downed the glass of fruit juice poured for her. 'It's true about tropical nights,' she joked determinedly. 'And it is time I went home. I know we haven't discussed that openly before but ...'

'You're damned right we haven't.'

She swallowed. 'We both knew I couldn't stay for ever and ... and I'd like to see Max,' she threw in for good measure.

'Tough!' Dane answered softly. 'You know most girls

learn at their mother's knee that men don't like to be chased. Leave it. Don't make a fool of yourself.'

Claire went white and then red, meeting that cool, unapologetic scrutiny. If he was waiting for Max to appear here, she was never going to get away, and she was terrified of staying in case he guessed how she really felt. Nor could she tolerate to stand on the sidelines closing her eyes politely to the affair he was obviously planning with Mei Ling.

'We'll head into the National Park,' Dane continued smoothly. 'Come on, Claire, eat your breakfast.'

In half an hour he had her tucked willy-nilly into the jeep, ignoring her visible lack of enthusiasm. The rain forest was lush and damp, the well laid trails sprinkled by pools of sunlight, but Claire was unable to appreciate sights that usually kept her chattering. After a brief walk they came to the Emerald Pool, a grotto fed by a waterfall and possessed of quite unearthly beauty. Overhanging giant feathery ferns and wild orchids supplied a profusion of colour that stole her breath away, however.

'It's fantastic,' she agreed in the silence. 'I'm never going to forget this island.'

Dane regarded her narrowly. 'I came to a decision last night,' he drawled. 'You don't want the house turned into a hotel. I'm going to have it done up and I'll give it to you. You won't have to forget Dominica. You'll own a corner of it.'

She couldn't quite believe her ears, and she whirled round to face him. 'But I don't want you to give me the house!' she said in horror.

'You're getting it.' His strong jawline had an aggressive thrust. 'I just wanted you to know before we leave on the yacht. It's something you really want and you'd never have told me on your own. You don't like jewellery much, do you?'

She flushed unhappily. Dane had not once come back from Jamaica empty-handed. A diamond bracelet, a necklace and a ring languished in the box on her dressing-table. Jewels worth a king's ransom that she shrank from. It was as though Dane felt that he had to buy himself out of their short-lived relationship. One more symptom of the feelings he didn't have for her, and his own clear conviction that he had to somehow compensate her for sharing his bed, however briefly. And now he planned to hurl a house at her, too. 'They're lovely ...' She hesitated, reluctant to offend.

'If Max had given them to you, you'd have been delighted,' he interposed drily. 'But not me.'

She was curiously cold, in spite of the heat. 'You don't owe me anything, Dane.'

'I just want you to be happy.'

She flung him a bitter smile. 'It can't be bought.'

'You're still having the house,' he delivered squarely. 'It'll be put in your name.'

'Damn you, I don't want it!' she repeated angrily.

He looked at her coldly, so coldly that she shuddered. 'Max might. I take it you haven't heard from him yet?'

The insinuation was so unbelievably insulting, she almost choked on her bitterness. He was gift-wrapping her for Max. It was incredible. Only Dane would have been capable of such a gesture. He would rest easy only when she was restored to Max and his conscience was sated. Unutterably humiliated now, Claire could feel hysteria closing over her like a suffocating blanket.

'Not yet,' she answered shakily.

Dane, misinterpreting her evident emotiom, folded his

arms round her in a move that was so disgustingly big brotherly and asexual that she felt violent. 'I'm sure you will,' he soothed. 'If you don't, I'll get in touch with him.'

In disbelief, her palms lodged against his chest to push him firmly away. 'Don't bother!' she snapped.

'When I said I could contact him, I only meant that I could explain,' Dane replied aggressively.

'Explain what?' Her green eyes blazed her outrage. 'What would you tell him? How would you describe me now? One owner, well maintained, complete new body? Maybe you'd like to run an ad in the paper to flog me to the highest bidder? My God, I despise you for this!' Biting back a tearing sob she turned her back on him, the sound of footsteps crunching from the mouth of the trail behind them.

'I think it's time we got back,' Dane said without expression. But he was pale beneath his golden tan, doubtless angered by her uncontrolled outburst and her lack of gratitude. As she realised how perilously close she had come to revealing her real feelings, she suppressed a stark quiver of relief. 'I don't think I ought to join you on the yacht. I could go home from here.'

'You're still my responsibility, Claire.'

She cringed from such brutal candour. 'No, I'm my own. You're really not much more liberated than Adam, are you?'

'You're different from the kind of women I'm used to. More vulnerable,' he replied grimly.

She had not required the information. He would not have been wet nursing Mei Ling in the aftermath of an affair. But he would not have been landed with a memory of her as a child—a child, a teenager and a young woman who had inspired a protective instinct that was not easily overcome.

The Kirbys were still in their rooms when they got back, and on the upper landing Dane turned to say, 'Get your maid to pack for you, Claire. We might as well leave here after lunch.'

For a flight to Jamaica where the yacht awaited them. A cruise was to follow, stopping off at various pleasure spots. By the end of that she would be even more savaged by Dane's emotional immunity to her. Add Mei Ling and she could end up ready to throw herself overboard. She wanted to leave now. It would be much harder to think up an excuse on the yacht. Yet wasn't such determination now likely to look suspicious in itself? She didn't want Dane to suspect that Mei Ling's arrival was driving her away, for of course it wasn't as simple as that.

Hannah gave her her mail while she was reluctantly packing. She sat down to read the two letters. There was a ten-line note from Randy, asking when she would be back in London and ready to introduce her to Dane.

'Curiosity is killing me,' she added as a postscript.

The other was from Maisie and it elevated Dane to sainthood. She wrote to tell Claire that Dane had arranged for their cottage to be repaired and modernised. She had finished reading and was staring unhappily into space when the solution to her plight came to her. If Dane believed that one of those letters came from Max, he could hardly pressure her into remaining.

She found him in his bedroom. 'I needed to talk to you in private,' she essayed at his questioning glance. 'I've heard from Max and I want to go back to London.'

He eyed her composed face assessingly. She stood blade-straight, a soft smile pinned to her lips in lieu of excitement. It crossed her mind humourlessly that she ought to have gone on stage.

'Immediately?' he queried shortly. 'Don't you think

that's a little indecently premature? What did he write? "Come home, all's forgiven"?' His scorn was palpable. 'I'd like to meet the guy first.'

Flames of pink lit her cheeks at his tone. 'How very civilised. Unfortunately, neither I nor Max would enjoy that, and my relationship with him is none of your business.'

'No, we're just two people who accidentally shared a bed on a few occasions, not married people,' Dane qualified with carrying sibilance. 'If you were my wife, I'd feel differently, wouldn't I?'

At that instant she did hate him for employing that rapier tongue upon her. 'Would you?'

He sprawled down lazily along the faded window-seat, raising one knee. 'You seem to have it in your head that I want rid of you. I don't want you fleeing back to England because you feel you have to. I'd prefer you to deliberate carefully about what you're doing first.'

'I don't need to deliberate, Dane. I'm not a silly teenager, although you like to treat me like one. I'm a woman,' she stated with quiet dignity.

'That did penetrate during one of those accidental brushes in the dark.' His retaliation was smooth. 'But you're not the same woman you were a few months ago, and I can't believe after the way you responded to me that you still want Max to the same extent.'

She bore his ungentlemanly reminder with tortured calm. 'There is a subtle distinction between love and sex.'

Vibrant blue eyes zeroed in on her consideringly. 'And I was the corrupting influence who taught you the distinction. Correct?'

'It doesn't matter any more,' she stressed with sudden unsteadiness. 'And I don't know why you're making this so unpleasant, unless it's because you've decided that four weeks isn't long enough for this fake marriage to last!'

'I don't give a damn what's said in the papers!' he raked back with contempt. 'But I think you're being childish. You're not going to be free to marry Max for a long time. There's no need for haste. If he's still interested in you, he'll wait.'

'Maybe I don't want to wait.'

His shrewd gaze shimmered. 'OK,' he capitulated abruptly, unexpectedly. 'You can leave today if you like, but I want to know where you are the minute you land in London. Then you can get on with your life and make a mess of it if you want to.'

'I started doing that the day I asked you to marry me!' she informed him curtly and slammed out of the room. He had only put up those arguments against her leaving to conceal his relief. Just for a tiny moment she had almost believed he really wanted her to stay. But his reluctance had merely been a polite pretence.

Hannah came to her room when she didn't appear at lunch. 'Dane tells me you're leaving.'

'You can't be surprised.' Claire was rehanging garments in the wardrobe. Trailing home designer leisure wear and cases of glamorous evening clothes was a waste of energy. 'You must have realised it wasn't a normal marriage.'

Hannah's broad face was openly troubled. 'I can't deny that, but Dane's very attached to you, Claire. He's made an enormous effort to please you over the past weeks.'

The hint of rebuke disconcerted her. 'You don't understand——' she began.

'I have eyes and ears. Look at that jewellery you never wear,' Hannah invited drily. 'If that isn't a kick in the teeth I don't know what is. I don't know what happened between you, and it's not my affair, but Dane has taken the separate bedrooms without a murmur, and that amazes me.'

It would have amazed Claire too, had it not been Dane's choice. She was feeling dizzy again and she lowered herself down on to the foot of the bed. 'He feels guilty,' she whispered miserably. 'And I don't want his guilt, or his gifts.'

There was a lengthy silence during which Hannah paced over to the window. 'I don't care what you say. Dane's not riled by conscience. There have been times I've wished he was, but he's not that scrupulous,' she conceded wryly. 'He finds it hard to show his feelings. He tends to make up for it by buying presents. That doesn't make his generosity questionable. He married you. He must have cared for you. I really never thought Dane would marry but when it was you, well ... I did feel it might work.'

Claire breathed in slowly until the light-headedness receded. What was wrong with her? Anxiety? Blood pressure?

'Dane married me because I asked him to,' she confided with a choked laugh. 'So that I could qualify to inherit my grandfather's estate. Now will you believe me when I tell you that Dane will be relieved to be released from what he finds a very onerous responsibility?'

Hannah had spun round, her face perplexed. 'So that's why!'

'Yes.' Doggedly she got up again to resume packing. 'I'm not entitled to his generosity. I already owe him more than I could repay in a lifetime.'

'But you love him. If you leave, you'll never know whether or not he could have started to care for you,' Hannah protested.

Claire's strained smile was a plea for understanding. 'He cares, Hannah, but he doesn't love me and why should he? I couldn't hold a candle to the sort of woman he's attracted by.' Her voice sliced off before she broke down. 'Don't you see that he'd blame himself for the way I feel, too? Please don't make this any harder for me than it already is.'

Randy opened the door, still talking animatedly to someone to one side of her. She surveyed Claire and her three cases in forgivable astonishment. Then absolute fury glittered in her huge blue eyes. 'That bastard!' she pronounced, and enveloped Claire in a cloud of musky perfume and sympathy and a breathless monologue on the evils of the male sex, with not a question on the horizon.

Dane's reputation had gone before him. Not for one moment did Randy doubt that Claire's descent hinged upon Dane's reputation as a womaniser. It was some minutes before the male, left to hover in the hall forgotten, entered the lounge.

Claire stilled as recognition darted through her. 'Gilles?'

Randy relayed the pair of them an amused glance and laughed. 'That's right. You two have already met?'

'Not really,' Claire muttered, suddenly wondering what she had blithely walked into.

'Not for very long,' Gilles le Freneau drawled mockingly. 'Randy and I occasionally work together. I'm a photographer. I live in the apartment on the top floor of this building.'

The proverbial coin dropped. Gil. The male Randy called Gil and was in love with. She had mentioned him several times in letters. He had clearly known about her friendship with Randy that day he had gone out of his way to speak to her and Hannah.

Randy sighed. 'Gil, I . . .'

He inclined his dark head. 'I'm going,' he teased. 'If I stayed, my sins would very likely be linked with Dane's.'

'I'm sorry, I seem to have——' Claire listened to the thud

of the front door. 'I shouldn't have landed on you like this. It was just so late and I couldn't face a hotel.'

Randy gave her an affectionate hug. 'Gil and I don't sleep together,' she said frankly. 'You didn't disturb us. We had a meal out because he said he was at a loose end.'

Viewing the grim light in her friend's eyes at that confession, she registered that the path of true love ran no smoother for her.

'We're really just friends,' she continued. 'He gave up switching on the Gallic charm ages ago. Would you like a drink? I know I would.'

Claire settled into Randy's spare room with ease. They had always had the kind of friendship that neither distance nor time lapses altered, and within the first week she found a job. Ironically, it came courtesy of Gilles.

He was a frequent visitor to the flat and when he learnt that she was looking for a job he viewed her with lancing amusement, but tactfully made no comment. A couple of days later, however, he called in to leave a phone number with her.

'John's an archaeologist. I did some photographic work for his current book. He's looking for an assistant to help him put together his material,' he said. 'His last one got bored with the isolation and left to work in an office. I mentioned your name. He suggested you ring if you're interested.'

John Hawthorne was a portly man in his fifties with a pleasant warmth of manner, and he offered her the job at their informal interview. He showed her the tiny office off the library of his townhouse and the typewriter that she felt confident of mastering for the few letters he would require of her. She also decided to enrol in night classes.

She tried to count her blessings then. It was infinitely preferable to have left Dane with all flags flying. He was content to think her reunited with Max and she was lucky to have a job. It mightn't last for ever but John would give her a good reference when he no longer required her services. The first few weeks of severance crawled past.

In low moments, she had a habit of staring out of her office window. It overlooked a walled garden and snowdrops were pushing their heads up bravely in the shelter of a wall despite the white carpet of a heavy ground frost. Dane was still whooping it up in the Caribbean with a variety of female companions. He had been photographed partying on the yacht. As sure as God made little apples Dane was not anywhere gazing out of a window watching snowdrops grow!

'If you ever need anything,' he had emphasised before she got on the plane, 'call me.'

And what would he do if she did and told him that she couldn't eat, couldn't sleep, would never have believed that there was this much pain in loving? But of course she wouldn't. At Christmas she would write. Christmas was a comfortable distance away. She might be capable of putting pen to paper by then.

She had sent a note of her address to Lew Harrison, receiving a reply by return of post that icily offered her an allowance per month which was more than her present salary would give her in an entire year. She had written back to say she was working and self-sufficent. At least she had made someone's day of recent! A tense smile fleeted across her lips. She had called in at the doctor's the day before yesterday on a much more enlightening mission, although she hadn't known it at the time.

She had been half-way through a careful delivery of her dizzy spells, her poor appetite and feeling like the worst of malingerers when the doctor had cut in to say, 'Forgive me, but is it possible that you could be pregnant?'

Claire had halted mid-flow. No, it hadn't occurred to her. Not once had it occurred to her, and her periods had often tended to be irregular during times of particular stress, so she hadn't paid any heed to the absence of one until the doctor drew her attention to the fact.

The possibility had shattered her initially. Old wives' tale or not, she had never credited that two nights in a man's arms could lead to such far-reaching consequences. And the news that she had to await the results of a test for confirmation had filled her with raw impatience.

John called in to remind her that she had asked if she could finish early. 'You'd better hurry,' he said, checking his watch.

She had to wait ages to see the doctor. Her nerves were stretched by the time she finally got into the surgery. Ten minutes later she floated out on air. The knowledge that she carried Dane's child inside her was a guilty source of joy, for she had no doubt how he would react to such a bombshell. Her delight, however, was soon equal to blocking out that momentary sense of discomfiture. She had finally discovered something capable of keeping her sane. There would be no more sleepless nights or scratchy meals. No more wallowing in a bottomless pit of self-pity for what she couldn't have. All of a sudden, she couldn't stop smiling!

CHAPTER EIGHT

'What do you mean, now you've got something to look forward to?' Randy still looked in need of resuscitation, her carrying voice piercing Claire's ears so that she almost winced. 'Are you out of your tiny mind? Life is just about to open up for you and you get a stab in the back like this . . . it doesn't bear thinking about!' she muttered feelingly, sinking down on the telephone seat.

Claire stifled her irritation. 'The baby, or the life that was opening up?' she teased. 'Honestly, I'm delighted.'

Randy glanced up. 'You came in here as white as a sheet.'

'The lift made me feel sick,' Claire admitted ruefully.

Randy shook her head. 'You really are happy about it. How can you be?' she demanded. 'Who wants to be stuck with a baby after the shortest marriage on record?'

Claire straightened her shoulders. 'I do and now you've said your piece, would you mind if we dropped the subject?'

She went into her room before her tactless friend could further detract from her pleasure. Randy had recently been plotting and planning to try and persuade Claire into accompanying her to parties and the like. To Randy, a pregnancy now, when her marriage was over bar the shouting, was a disaster. For Claire, a serene and softened smile on her mouth as she examined her still slender profile in the mirror, it was redemption. She couldn't have Dane but she could have his child.

'I'm sorry about last night,' Randy said over breakfast the next day, her eyes rueful. 'I put my foot where my mouth is. I thought about it. I talked it over with Gilles.'

Claire's lashes swept up. 'You did what?'

Her friend groaned. 'He's my best friend next to you.'

'I wish you hadn't told him.'

'I guess we could have said you were comfort-eating when you expanded,' Randy retorted sarcastically.

Claire smiled. 'I wasn't planning on staying here.'

'Start planning. Things have to change.' Randy had a managerial air about her now. 'First though ... the only conclusion I came to was that he must be one hell of a guy.'

Claire's green eyes filmed over.

'But I hate getting maudlin over the breakfast table,' added Randy hastily. 'How do you intend to tell him?'

'I don't.'

'Claire!'

'I know him. He doesn't want children.' Claire tilted her chin. 'And it would devastate him.'

Randy regarded her dimly. 'It does take two, you know. I assume he knew what he was doing ...'

Claire was thinking back to their wedding day. No, he had not quite known what he was doing, and he had not expected her to be quite the innocent she had proved to be. 'He would feel responsible,' she murmured tautly. 'God, I couldn't take that again! Don't you understand?'

'I'm trying ... really I am, but that was one weird relationship you had.'

Dane had his freedom back. He was probably thriving on it. As far as he was concerned, she too was perfectly happy. Why rock the boat? Hadn't she already upset his life enough? Becoming a father would not be something he could brush aside and forget, and one of the facets she had always loved in Dane was his unfettered honesty. She didn't want him to be forced to lie and pretend to protect her feelings. The baby would be an unwelcome surprise that would unleash a whole host of complications. Anyway, could anyone in their right mind imagine Dane warming to a baby?

She rubbed her brow tiredly. 'The baby is my responsibility and we'll get by without hanging on anyone's sleeve.'

Randy bit back a tirade. 'Dane has got so much money it wouldn't make any difference to him if you accepted that allowance his solicitor offered.

'Why should Dane pay, when I was never his wife?' she parried stubbornly.

'Did I hear that right?' Randy hesitated. 'I mean, it is his? Yes, of course it is, but really, Claire, you're being very . . . secretive.'

Claire had no doubts about the decision not to tell Dane. She loved him too much to think of inflicting such news upon him in the name of honesty. It wouldn't be fair. Dane would halt the divorce proceedings she presumed Lew had begun. He would take on an obligation he had never wanted, and deep down inside he would be stifling his anger.

The weeks drifted past and became months. Spring passed by and then early summer. She continued to work for John and indeed she was on a shopping trip for him when she bumped into Gilles one morning in Harrods. He set her back from him, smiling. 'A most prophetic meeting,' he teased. 'It's Randy's birthday next week and I'm at a loss.'

She grinned. 'I don't believe you.'

His dark brows quirked. 'It stopped you breezing past.'

'I don't breeze anywhere these days.' She felt like a barge in her floral cotton dress and flat shoes on this warm day.

He just laughed and anchored a careless arm round her shoulders. 'I think I'll take you out to lunch.'

'John's expecting me back.'

Gilles stared down at her. 'John works you through your lunch hour? He has no appreciation for the clock,' he retorted crisply. 'And you're not being very sensible doing that in your condition.'

'Don't!' she groaned.

'Don't what?'

Her face was full of unconscious appeal. 'Mention it. Randy makes such a fuss, and John *isn't* working me through my lunch hour. He sends me out because he thinks fresh air is good for me.'

Gilles sighed. 'I suppose an old bachelor hasn't a clue how to treat a pregnant woman. I'd say exercise is about the last thing you need right now.'

He was right. She was hot and harassed and her back was sore. She was at that stage of pregnancy where she felt as if she had been pregnant for years. She let him lead her out to the crowded pavement.

'We never get the chance to talk,' he remarked when he had finally found a cab. 'You disappear when I'm around.'

Perhaps her tact had been a bit heavy, she construed. Randy was in love with him. And Gilles? Gilles had an ability to screen his emotions in a way similar to Dane's.

'It's not my business,' he began, 'but . . .'

She took a deep breath. 'But nothing. I don't discuss Dane with anyone, Gilles.'

He persisted regardless. 'You're not leading a practical life-style.'

'I'm happy and healthy,' Claire answered bitingly. 'And one-parent families are not exactly rare.'

He studied her tightly folded hands. 'I wish I understood, but however——' he produced a careless smile '——I'll say no more for the moment. Instead I'll tell you why I'm in the mood to celebrate.'

She looked at him enquiringly as they crossed the

pavement together. 'I've just bought a ring for Randy,' he confided spreading open the door of the restaurant.

'Does she know?'

He shook his head as they were shown to a table.

'Is a respectable proposal accompanying it?' Claire dared, awake to the possibility that there mightn't be.

He laughed. 'But of course, and it's probably the only one I've ever made,' he confessed cheerfully.

She smiled and leant forward to grasp his hand. 'I'm glad,' she said.

So preoccupied were they that they neither of them noticed the tall redhead rising to her feet at a corner table, an expression of stunned disbelief freezing her features. Claire was just accepting the menu when Zelda stalked over to them.

'You poisonous little bitch,' she hissed, with no thought of lowering her voice. 'With him, of all people!'

Claire flinched in startled collision with Zelda's angrily accusing eyes. But the older girl awaited no reply. She sped back to the table she had been sharing with another woman. Gilles had already risen again.

Claire shakily drew breath. 'Do you mind if we go?' she mumbled, hot with embarrassment.

'She'll tell him,' she sighed in the cab he had procured.

Gilles cursed. 'It was my fault. I should have known better than to take you out in public. I forgot who I was and who you are by doing so, and I wouldn't blame Dane for being angry. My apologies, Claire, but I'd prefer to take you back to John's.'

It was what she preferred, too. Had Zelda noticed that she was pregnant? She could hardly have failed to do so. Hadn't she been delighted by her disappearance from Dane's life? Then she would enjoy telling him what a lucky escape he had had.

The afternoon hummed past while she worked. At about four she heard John speaking to another man next door in his library, and when he came into her office she was slightly surprised, for when he had a visitor he generally forgot about work. He smiled. 'Someone to see you, Claire.'

Dane topped him by half a head, immediately visible to her shocked gaze. After John had gone, he remained poised by the filing cabinet just staring at her where she had frozen upright by her desk. His magnificent blue eyes zeroed in on her pale face only briefly for his attention quickly lodged on the rest of her. He went a whiter shade of pale beneath the dark, burnished gold of his tan.

'You're pregnant!' He practically whispered it, as if it was something decent people didn't say out loud.

He was riveted to the spot. She wished she could just shut her eyes and disappear, a flaming and anguish-filled embarrassment afflicting her. There was nothing remotely cute or dainty about her now. She had the sex appeal of a blimp in a cotton tent.

He braced a not very steady, long-fingered hand on the cabinet. 'Very pregnant,' he added dazedly.

He left Randy behind in degrees of shock. He had entered blazing with ice-cold temper, and right in front of her eyes it had drained out of him, along with his usual hard self-assurance. The strident ring of the phone broke the terrible silence.

'Claire?' It was Randy and she sounded frantic. 'Gil has done the most dreadful thing. I can't tell you how sorry I am. He went to see Dane and told him where to find you, and God only knows what else he told him! I'm sorry.'

'It's all right. He's here. I'll speak to you later.'

'You won't be speaking to anyone but me later,' Dane contradicted, closing the space between them suddenly to remove the receiver from her hand and drop it down on to the cradle. The angles of his hard cheekbones were sharper and there was a whipcord edge to his leanness now. Obviously, his constant partying had to have had some effect even on his tough constitution, she told herself miserably. 'I guess I never thought I'd end up being in Gilles' debt for anything.' He muttered wryly.

Her now shoulder-length hair obscured her profile. She was not up to a scene and yet the very sight of him was a tormenting pleasure. 'You shouldn't have come.'

'If we follow that back and say I shouldn't have gone to Adam's funeral, we might be on the right track,' he delivered with unexpected savagery. 'Gilles said you needed me.'

'Like hell I need you!' she spat through a veil of angry, despairing tears.

A pair of strong arms enclosed her rigid body. 'Stop it,' he urged as if he was soothing a cross child. 'All these months you let me think you were with Max, and Gilles tells me there's nobody on the scene. No damned wonder!'

His gaze was pinned to the swell of her stomach which was keeping them apart, his fascination naked. Indeed if he had looked at any other part of her in the past minutes, she had missed it. Her small hands coiled into fists. 'Dane, please go away!' she sobbed.

Instead he pressed her down into her swivel chair and squatted down at her level, tugging her hands down from her face and holding them in a fierce grip. 'This must have come as a shock,' he murmured tautly. 'Hell, I'm still in shock. However, you've had months to get used to it. Do you——' his hesitation was uncharacteristic '—want it? I never realised it could be that easy ... no, don't listen to what I'm saying, I don't know what I'm saying yet.'

The fierce resentment in her dissipated. She was tempted to bury her hands in his wind-tousled hair. She wanted so badly to hold him close. But she was locked inside herself by comprehension of how he had to feel. He must be thinking someone had cursed him at Adam's funeral. She was like a disaster zone in his vicinity! Everything that could have gone wrong *had* gone wrong, and this last revelation was clearly one he hadn't even thought about.

'I'm pleased about it,' she muttered, ashamed in the face of his response to show more enthusiasm.

Supple fingers turned up her chin. 'When it's cost you Max?' he derided.

So that was what he thought! Deep colour banished her pallor. His hand dropped away and her lips parted, but Dane was already speaking again. 'Whatever else you think of me, I care about you. I care about what happens to you.'

Go on, she encouraged inwardly, make me feel even more like an albatross round your neck. Caring could never be loving. Caring belonged with weighty words like duty and responsibility and obligation. Claire had had sufficient experience of those at Ranbury to know how demanding and ultimately unsatisfactory they could be for the giver.

'You don't understand,' she forced out the charge. 'So you can stop feeling guilty. Max——' She swallowed hard, the last bolt on her pride shot, but it would be wickedly unjust to leave Dane believing that her pregnancy had deprived her of Max. 'Max has someone else.' She studied a button on his shirt. 'Even before Grandfather died. I didn't know. He just didn't get round to telling me.'

She heard his breath escape audibly. He sprang upright without the forgivably furious exclamation she was waiting for. 'You've got every right to be angry,' she continued doggedly. 'I should never have married you before I had a chance to speak to him face to face. And when I think about it calmly . . . after the way you threw all those clothes and things at me . . . well, you might have done something for

Maisie and Sam if I'd asked you.'

She dug a hanky from her pocket and wiped her eyes.

'Just think of all the fun I'd have missed.' Dane had his back turned to her, big broad shoulders taut beneath his shirt. 'There wasn't any letter on Dominica, was there?'

'No.' She stifled a sob. 'All of this has been my fault.'

'Come on.' He swung round with sudden purpose. 'I'll take you home.'

It was clear when they entered the library that John already knew Dane's identity. His beam of approval was only lightened by his disappointment that she would not be returning—an assumption she said nothing about in Dane's presence.

'What did Gilles tell you?' she demanded as soon as they were inside the Rolls, which had been waiting out on the street.

He gave one of his annoyingly careless shrugs. But he still looked unusually tense. 'Not much. He got in before Zelda just to straighten out any misunderstanding there might have been, and he told me that there was no man around that he knew of.'

Gilles had stupidly implied that she was in some sort of trouble and Dane had taken the bait. His silence worked on her overstretched nerves and it was a relief when they completed the short drive to the flat. As she fumbled with her key Dane ran a finger along the nameplate on the front door. 'M Blair. Miranda Blair. When I checked that address you gave Lew, I assumed the M stood for Max,' he revealed softly. 'I never did get his surname.'

He had thought she had been living with Max and he had been content with that. It spoke volumes for his attitude towards her. She cursed Gilles for his high-handed interference between them. Had he known the circumstances of their parting he might have understood that he had done neither of them a good turn.

'Where's your flatmate? The unfortunate who's settling on Gilles for a husband?' he queried sarcastically in the hall.

'I like Gilles. He's never been anything other than kind to me,' she protested. 'And Randy's out. She rang from a callbox.'

'Which is your room? 'With his usual aplomb, Dane pushed open doors. 'Hell, do I need to ask? Who else would have a photo of the Fletchers *en famille* by the bed? I bet you haven't heard a word from one of them since you took off into the wide blue yonder.'

She shut the door. 'You'd be wrong. Sandra called in one evening because she was down in London.'

'And here you are roughing it, pregnant and deserted. I can imagine that went down beautifully,' Dane commented coldly, his bright gaze condemning. 'I gather you let her think I ditched you.'

'We didn't discuss it.' She straightened her back tiredly, overtly conscious of his hard scrutiny. She felt so ugly that she wanted to curl up and die, and she wished he'd stop staring as if she had sprouted wings. Doubtless he was still trying to adjust to the idea that he was shortly to become a father.

'I'll help you pack.'

She frowned. 'Pack?'

It was an unnecessary question. Dane had self-sacrifice written all over him. He was ready to assume responsibility again. Inwardly she squirmed. He had to hate her for this. 'I'm sorry . . . I really am sorry.'

'I want the baby, Claire.'

'Once more with conviction,' she quipped wretchedly.

'If you say you're sorry once more, I'll . . .' His roughened drawl cut off mid-sentence as he surveyed the defeated aspect of her strained eyes. 'Max is out of it, Claire. Isn't it time you faced up to the fact that the only two people concerned now are you and me?' he enquired drily.

He still believed she was dumb enough to crave another man when she was carrying his child! However, that was safer than letting him guess the truth when the truth would make him feel uncomfortable.

'How do you feel?'

Emptied, mortified and as welcome as a snow shower in June! 'I'm OK, it's not a sickness, you know!' she fended waspishly.

'Does nothing for your temper,' Dane hazarded unprovoked, something gleaming in his measuring appraisal that she couldn't interpret. 'I could say a lot of things you wouldn't believe but instead I'll be straight. I've reached the end of my patience with you, Claire. You're coming with me and you're going to remain my wife. If you don't, I'll take that baby from you.'

The blood chilled in her veins. Encountering cool sapphire eyes she trembled. 'But you don't want . . .'

'How would you know?' His interruption was crushing. 'So I once said I had no great desire for kids. The situation's different when my child is only a few weeks off being born.'

Her curling lashes hid her unhappy eyes. He couldn't deceive her to that extent. He would prefer to use pressure to convince her that he too wanted the baby. So it was silly of her to be frightened even for a moment by his threat. He was being cruel to be kind. She could have smote him dead for just being what he was. A breathtakingly beautiful male viewing his most unbeautiful and most unwanted and very pregnant wife. Fate was very cruel fishing up Dane now when she was round as a barrel, she reflected bitterly. Women didn't have unplanned babies in Dane's world. He had to be thinking about that, grimly wishing he hadn't let his temper get the better of him, and it was lowering, unbelievably lowering.

'I didn't want you to find out like this.'

His scrutiny was cold. 'You didn't want me to find out at all.'

'I thought you'd be happier that way.'

He swore, and in his heart she knew he had to agree with her. He couldn't want to return to the charade of a marriage which he had already put behind him, over so ignominious a stumbling block as a baby. In some cases, ignorance could be bliss.

Her hands flickered together and finally linked. 'I'd never have asked you to marry me if I'd known how ... what are you laughing at?'

He grinned. 'I've missed having you around.'

Her almost-smile ebbed instantly. 'You don't need to say things like that.'

'All right, I didn't miss you. I now feel trapped. Is that what you want to hear?' he raked in exasperation. 'What makes you think that I'd be trapped by any situation that I didn't like?'

Very easy to say. His wishes had had no effect on her conception, and with the baby so close to being born, there was very little else he could say. Dane was a positive thinker. He wasn't the type to groan about what couldn't be changed. 'I think it would be better if you left me alone,' she stated tightly.

'And I wander off and neglect to recall that I have a child somewhere? What the hell gives you the right to make that kind of demand?'

Startled, she clashed with the warning glitter of his challenging gaze. He tilted his head back and sighed. 'Look, this isn't getting us anywhere fast. Why don't I take you out to dinner?'

Bewilderment held her fast. 'I . . . I don't think I could face going out tonight.' She bit her lip. 'But if you like, you can eat here.'

'You look beat. I don't want to put you to any trouble.'

Claire surveyed him wearily. 'It won't be any trouble. I'd like to get changed. The lounge,' she muttered, 'is at the foot of the hall.'

After a brief but refreshing wash, she slipped on the caftan Randy had brought her from Tunisia a few months earlier. She felt immediately more comfortable in its concealing folds. While she was dressing she heard Randy come in, and when she left her room her friend's throaty laughter carried from the lounge. Tight-mouthed, Claire retreated from the door. Clearly Randy had succumbed to curiosity and joined Dane. By the sound of it, her view of him was already changing.

'Need a hand?' Randy put her head round the kitchen door a half-hour later, her face still alight with a smile. 'I didn't realise how late it was getting and I still have to get changed. Gil's taking me somewhere special tonight,' she confided, watching Claire remove a pair of steaks from beneath the grill. 'I do understand, all of a sudden,' she threw in abruptly.

'Understand?'

Randy looked defensive. 'He has extraordinary charm. I didn't expect to like him. You should forgive him, Claire. What's one . . .' she faltered, 'slip to a guy like that?'

'What indeed?' Claire concealed her annoyance over Randy's quick conversion.

'He's gorgeous.'

'I noticed.'

'Sarcasm doesn't become you,' Randy giggled then. 'I gave him a drink and told him how quietly you'd been living. He's very easy to talk to, isn't he?'

And with that damning remark Randy skipped off to her room where she could be heard frantically slamming through drawers. Claire seethed. Why hadn't she broken that twosome up? Dane was incredibly good at getting information out of people.

He strolled through to the small dining annexe as soon as she called him. It shook her how much pleasure she earned from his simple presence, shook her that she had been childishly jealous of Randy's response to him. She wished so many impossible things: that this had just been a visit she could enjoy rather than the prelude to an argument. Sometimes Dane needed protecting from himself and this was one of those times.

He took a seat with a provocative smile. 'Did you really have a photo of me tacked inside your locker at school?'

She thrust the salad bowl at him with unnecessary force. 'It was fashionable to have a pin-up.'

'You were fifteen,' he said ruefully.

She flushed. 'There was no one else to compete.'

'Nasty,' he reproved.

'Well, it's true!' Warming to the subejct in self-defence, she persisted, 'You were the only person who paid me a blind bit of attention at Ranbury.'

'Carter should have been looking ahead.'

Against her volition she giggled and then asked, 'Did Zelda go and see you?'

'Phoned.' He shrugged. 'Matt and she have separated. Did you know that?'

She shook her head.

'It was a mutual decision, and probably the best thing,' he allowed carelessly.

When they'd finished eating, he got up, staying her hands when she would have begun to clear the table. 'Can we talk about us now? I'll take you down to Wytchwood.

That's my house in Kent. You'll like it there. It's quiet.'

Claire went to shut the curtains, eager to put some space between them. She found it quite impossible to look at him and refuse him when every traitorous sense urged her to capitulate. To be with him on any terms at any cost. Oh, it would be so easy to give in after the long, empty months she'd laboured through, but if she did there would be a different agony to live with daily: Dane's essential indifference. Eventually he would begin to hate her for the situation. He was human, too. She couldn't bear to think of Dane hating her, but that was what happened when one partner felt trapped out of a sense of duty alone. He didn't want the baby and he didn't want her. For how long could he pretend otherwise?

Valiantly she breathed in. 'I'm not going anywhere with you, Dane. I thought I'd made that clear. You get on with your life and I'll get on with mine,' she delineated. 'As you can see, I've managed fine so far.'

'Like hell you have!' he countered harshly.

Wytchwood, she was thinking bitterly. His country estate. He probably had a woman in residence in the penthouse. They had broken the mould when Dane was made. That keen, analytical brain of his was matched by a frightening degree of ruthlessness.

He continued, unaffected by her rigidly turned back. 'Think of it as a fresh start. By the grace of God we're still married and you've got no one else in your life. Still, I guess hugging a ghost at night is much more your style. You'll never get a hairshirt that way.'

His taunt spun her round again. 'You think you just have to snap your fingers and people obey, don't you?'

A winged sable brow climbed. 'I think my wife does,' he murmured warningly.

'I'm not your wife!' she argued shakily. 'We were

separated. You're only still here because I'm pregnant. Why can't you at least be honest about that? I'm not so fragile. You feel responsible again.'

Instead of denying the charge he angled back his silvery head, ice-blue eyes striking off hers. 'And why not? Who else is responsible for you?'

The tiny hope she had had died, blurring the remainder of his speech. His code of honour, his very conviction that she was somehow helpless, was compelling him into something that was all wrong.

'Since you're in such an unreasonable mood I'll skip the coffee,' he dropped. 'You can think over what I've said, and pack. I'll pick you up in the morning when you've calmed down and decided to stop playing Little Orphan Annie.'

Her lips parted. 'I . . .'

'No choices,' he ruled. 'You made your choice on Dominica. It was the last chance you'll ever get from my corner to decide your own future. I'm making this decision for you.'

That was so horrendously arrogant even for Dane, she was close to speechless. 'You don't have any rights over me!'

His eloquent mouth twitched. 'Why don't you look in a mirror? You've got a husband.'

'Ha!' she slotted in with contempt and won herself a coldly inscrutable stare.

'And a baby on the way.' There it was again. He was throwing it in her teeth. If her stomach had been flat Dane would have been gone by now with an airy wave. 'I'll see you at ten tomorrow,' he completed impatiently.

'I won't answer the door,' she replied.

As he unlatched it he looked back at her, his expression predatory. 'Course you will, Claire. You'd be too scared I'd kick it down and get the neighbours talking.'

And with that he departed. Shooting the bolt home gave

her small satisfaction, although she had to unlock it again after she had tidied the kitchen. Randy could hardly be locked out of her own home.

A clean, civilised break. On Dominica she had believed that was possible. Now it seemed unlikely. His anger was encouraging him to act impetuously, she told herself. Perhaps overnight he would begin to see the worth of what she had advocated. Only unhappiness could result from Dane doing something he didn't want to do. It would take a remarkable degree of saintlike unselfishness for such an unequal marriage to work. Love Dane or not, Claire didn't see him managing such a feat of endurance over a long haul. He would grow to resent her. But dear heaven, she reflected tearfully when she ended up pacing the floor in the early hours, if she had thought differently, she would have snatched at the offer with both hands.

CHAPTER NINE

'He was away by seven?' Randy breathed in dismay.

Claire managed to raise an amused brow as she passed her friend a fresh cup of tea and coiled back into her corner of the settee. 'Nothing's changed.'

Randy groaned disagreement. 'Everything's changed. He obviously wants you back.'

Darn Randy and her taste for happy endings! She had drifted home around dawn, still semi-hypnotised with her ring. In the radius of such delight, Claire felt a wet blanket. 'Because of the baby. Would you want that to be the sole basis of your marriage?' she asked bluntly.

'No.' Randy had gone pink, her aura of pushy persuasion somewhat dimmed. 'Then what are you going to do?'

'I'll let him support me.' Her soft mouth twisted. 'That ought to satisfy his sense of obligation.'

'How to damn with faint praise,' Randy sighed. 'He mightn't be as anti-kids and commitment as you think. Take Gil as an example. He married Dane's mother for her money.' Her eyes shadowed. 'He hasn't told me any lies about what he was like when he was younger. Like Dane, he was pretty wild. But he's changed.'

Claire could only guess what that reference to Eleanor had cost her friend in terms of pride. 'Believe me, if Dane changes it won't be on my account,' she murmured. 'And he certainly doesn't need a wife for the reasons men usually need wives. He's got staff who take very efficient care of him and women, well . . . they come and go and that's how Dane likes it.'

In the interim of awkward silence the bell went twice in

quick succession. 'It must be for you,' Claire said. 'Dane won't be here until ten.'

Inordinately relieved to be released from the honesty session, Claire went to her room, since she was still clad in her cotton nightdress.

'Guess I'm early.' Dane's low-pitched drawl sent her spinning round from the window in visible confusion. He shut the door. 'Are you packed yet?'

Her fingers pressed against the tiny flickering pulse at the base of her throat. 'I'm not going anywhere, so I don't need to pack.'

His jaw clenched, his earlier half-smile evaporating. 'I thought we had all this out last night.'

She lowered her unhappy eyes. 'I'll accept that allowance Lew offered if it makes you feel better, and I'll be able to find a small house somewhere. That would be the most sensible solution.'

'Whoever told you I was sensible? And where's your ring?' Moving forward he trapped and turned up her bare left hand. 'Don't you feel embarrassed to run round like this with no wedding ring on?'

For tact, he took the biscuit! 'My fingers got fat like the rest of me!' she snapped and snatched her fingers back from his cool grasp. 'Don't you understand, Dane? No further sacrifices are necessary!'

His hard mouth curled. 'I'm not of the martyr ilk. Now why don't you get dressed? It's a beautiful day and you'll enjoy the drive down to the house.'

It was like beating her head up against a brick wall and she wanted it over with, wanted him gone before she started crying and Dane began to realise he had her exactly where he wanted her. So she yanked open the door. 'I'm not going anywhere with you, so you can go and do whatever you would have been doing if Gilles hadn't visited you yesterday!' she blazed shakily.

'I would have been working.'

'Really?' She raised a doubting, supercilious brow.

Tension sizzled in the air between them. 'I warned you,' he breathed softly and clamped a pair of firm hands to her non-existent waist and suddenly, quite unbelievably, lifted her into the air. Her mules fell off and she aimed a kick at him while he held her there. 'Put me down, Dane! Do you hear me?' she demanded.

'Shut up,' Dane said succinctly, bundling her half over his shoulder, but not before she had seen the pure, untamed glitter of purpose in his eyes. 'I wonder what gave you the crazy idea that I would listen to you being sensible the second time around. Once was enough.'

'Randy!' Claire wailed at the top of her lungs, pummelling at his back with her fists but she was all at the wrong angle, thanks to her stomach.

Dane was hauling open the front door. 'I'll send someone over for Claire's clothes later if you'd be kind enough to pack them,' he was saying.

Randy stood by in shock and steadily gathering mirth.

'I'll never forgive you for this,' Claire cried furiously in the lift. 'In my nightdress! You can't take me out of here in my nightdress. Now take me back! Don't you dare make an exhibition of me in public!'

'You're doing just fine on your own,' Dane gritted.

Struggling for control, she choked on a very unladylike epithet. Cooler air hit her as they left the lift. A retired couple, who lived in the flat below Randy's, were standing seemingly transfixed by the lift doors when she looked back. 'Dane,' she sobbed wrathfully in the fresh air. 'How could you do this to me?'

He stowed her determinedly in the rear seat of the Rolls and swung in beside her. Only the convulsed look on the chauffeur's face silenced her until the door slammed on them both.

'Well, if ever anybody got what they asked for,' Dane provoked, stretching out his long, lean legs in insolent relaxation, 'you have. Stop fussing and shut up. I'll buy you something to wear.'

'And then you will take . . . there's nowhere for me to get dressed!' she realised on a new tide of near tongue-tied rage.

'Little prude.' Dane lifted the phone to communicate with his driver.

'I think you've gone insane.' Claire thrust her hair off her damp brow in utter frustration. 'How dare you tell me to shut up?'

'I should have told you that a long time ago,' he murmured gently.

The rest of her recriminations were greeted by silence. When she eventually ran out of steam, Dane leant forward and opened the bar to extract a glass and what looked like fresh orange juice in a container. 'Thompson's compliments. He said Vitamin C would be good for you,' he advanced. 'But I don't reckon you need more energy.'

'It was the baby he was talking about.' She took the glass with an unsteady hand.

'He got driven down to the house last night to get things ready,' he continued. 'Once you're installed you'll be really comfortable there. Anyone would think I was threatening you with a prison sentence. I won't be there all the time.'

He sounded so cool and uninterested that her eyes pricked with tears. He'd forced her out of the apartment because he wasn't prepared to waste any more time discussing it.

He left the car in the vicinity of Bond Street. She curled up but she couldn't get very comfortable. An odd little ache in her back kept on niggling at her and she finally rested her head back with a cross mutter. Yes, she was cross. In fact, she was in a filthy mood. I won't be there all the time. No, indeed he wouldn't be! He'd be jetting about the globe, free to savour all the wicked, wanton pursuits he thrived upon and which she would read about in the papers. The world would turn full circle for her again and she'd still be on the outside looking in.

Dane was ages, and when he returned he was loaded down with carrier bags. 'We can stop once we get outside the city limits.'

'Nothing will fit,' she forecast.

'I'm not a complete bozo. I went to a maternity shop. The rest of you is still the same size, maybe even a bit thinner.' His appraisal was sharply critical and she shifted uncomfortably. 'The ladies were very helpful.'

'I just bet they were.' Huffily she rummaged in the bags. He cleared his throat. 'When's it due?'

'It?'

'Well, what do you expect me to call it?' he rasped impatiently.

'I'm sorry. Three weeks.' She stuck her feet into a pair of low-heeled leather mules, after several attempts.

'What do you want?'

'God doesn't take orders.'

He burst out laughing and then bent down to encircle one of her ankles with cool fingers. 'That's swollen like your fingers. Is that normal?'

She reddened. Her pacing last night wouldn't have helped. 'It's the heat, that's all.'

He didn't look quite convinced, but she basked in his ignorance of such matters. 'You won't be doing anything strenuous today,' he said after an awkward pause.

He had bought three dresses, each of them the last word in maternity chic, and all aimed at the current hot spell. True to his word he had the car pulled into a lay-by an hour later and with great amusement he climbed out, followed by his now poker-faced chauffeur. His sense of humour had awakened her own. She slid into the silky French knickers with a grin, ignoring the tights. Pulling the coolest looking of the dresses over her head, a crisp navy and white sundress, she stowed her nightie in one of the carriers and buzzed down the window to signal the all clear.

She borrowed his comb to tidy her hair. 'Your driver must think we're mad,' she muttered.

'I don't know. Wifenapping's fun.' Dane treated her to a lazy, even-tempered smile. 'Feel better?'

She nodded dutifully. Having achieved his objective, he could afford to smile. She stole a glance at his perfect profile, becoming a little greedy as she let her starved gaze slowly plot a course down over his superbly male physique, accepting the insidiously sweet stirrings of her own body in response.

'I got Thompson to fix a picnic,' he announced.

'A picnic?'

'Why not?' His tone was curt. 'I've never been on a picnic in my life, do you know that?'

She could have guessed, and the admission didn't imply to her that he was dying to fill the gap in experience. It was about noon when the car filtered off to minor roads, into a wooded area where it eventually stopped. The chauffeur solemnly produced a hamper and a rug from the boot.

It's part of the Wytchwood estate,' Dane informed her with a slanting grin. 'That's how I know about this place.'

He was so obviously set on his picnic plan that she smiled. Just being in the presence of all that vitality of his brightened her. Vibrations of sheer sensual enjoyment emanated from him and touched that cold spot in her heart. He was quite, quite irreplaceable, and she wished unhappily that she had been able to retain him as a friend. Only then she wouldn't have had the baby and, selfish or not, she was still gloriously happy about the child she carried. It was a part of him he couldn't deny her.

They only had to walk a couple of hundred yards before

they reached a sunny spot by the edge of the stream. 'Very
pretty,' she pronounced. 'Is the house far from here?'

He spread the rug. 'About a mile.'

She lowered herself down and kicked off her mules with
relief, while Dane stretched sensuously in the sunlight,
making her smile again. Opened, the hamper revealed a
wealth of sophisticated picnic fare.

'Thompson must have been very busy,' she whispered, in
awe of such delights in an outdoor setting.

'He's been hell to live with since I came back from the
Caribbean without you. He approved of you.' He uncorked
the bottle of champagne and extracted two glasses. 'If he
could have got candles in here, I dare say he would have,'
he mocked. 'He's a real romantic at heart. I know damned
fine that he thinks the split was over something I did. And
here you are, my wife, who left me for another man. A
midget, no less.'

'Dane,' she whispered.

He passed her a fluted crystal glass. 'To live in abject
poverty with her lover. I mean, no one would believe that
without thinking what a monster of depravity I must have
been,' he intoned sardonically. 'Still, one mustn't repine.'

'It wouldn't work, Dane,' she said very quietly. Tears
clogged her throat as the champagne bubbles tickled her
nose. 'And you don't owe me anything.'

Please, please, please make him stop trying to persuade
me! She wasn't a plaster saint. Every second she spent in his
company made denial all the more painful. It made her
wonder if it could really do so much harm to say yes . . . and
that was dangerous.

'Meaning that I'm not necessary now that you've
attained motherhood?'

Seared by his contempt, she paled and drank deep before
half whispering, 'Why can't you be honest?'

'Too much honesty can be risky.' His slow drawl carried

a perceptible chill of warning as he leant back on one elbow to watch her.

Claire unwrapped the crab mousse in its individual soufflé dishes.

'The problem won't go away,' he continued doggedly.

Her delicate profile washed with colour. 'A baby isn't a problem.'

'It is when you act as if I had nothing to do with its conception.'

She studied her mousse with fading appetite and put an absent hand to the base of her spine to massage her sore back. 'It was an accident.'

His jawline squared. 'The baby's going to love hearing that,' he gibed coldly.

She rammed down a terrible jolt of pain. He didn't have to be so literal. 'You've spent months being more visible than you've been in years, having a good time, because three wretched weeks of marriage frightened you half to death.'

'Four weeks,' he corrected pleasantly. 'It was your choice to leave.'

Yes, it had been. Without his love it had seemed the kindest and most fair decision to make. His gipsy life-style suited him and so did the Mei Lings who never demanded more than he was prepared to give. He didn't need anyone. The kind of intense, aching pleasure-pain she endured just being close to him lay within a range of emotions that he was immune to. But in spite of that inviolability he still knew what he ought to feel and he was clever enough to say and do what he conceived to be the right things. She sighed. 'I don't want you to be unhappy, Dane.'

His wolfish smile was larded with cynicism. 'What is happy, Claire? Oh, don't look at me like that,' he mocked. 'You're so innocent, sometimes I feel a hundred years old. A year ago you were happily planning your future with Max and I wasn't planning mine with anybody. All that's changed now. You can't turn back the clock. I tried. The one decent thing I did in the last decade and it turned out to be the stupidest thing I ever did!' Lush black lashes fanned up, throwing her into glancing contact with intensely blue eyes. 'Don't tell me you're happy now because I wouldn't believe you. You've got to shake this idea that marriages are made in heaven.'

'Ours certainly wasn't.' She let him refill her glass, still flinching from his blunt statement about how stupid he had been to marry her in the first place.

He cast her a cool smile. 'Neither was my parents' and it survived,' he stated with derisive challenge. 'And our marriage hasn't even had a proper trial yet. There's a lot of things I like about you. If we didn't crowd each other and develop too high expectations, we could survive too.'

He was staring down into her absorbed face and when he lazily angled his mouth down to capture her lips, one palm framing her cheekbone as he smoothly adjusted her weight against him, it seemed entirely natural. Her heart threatened to break free of her chest. The high voltage charge of sexual electricity she met sent her flat, boneless as a jellyfish and about as graceful as one stranded on the beach, she thought wretchedly as he lifted his head again. Eight months pregnant, too. She shrivelled with shame, certain it was her fault he had suddenly backed off.

He sat up, carefully distancing himself from her, she noted, and she was still all jittery and hot and cold with the hunger only he could ignite. He appeared cool, colour lying along his blunt cheekbones in a hard line, however, and a spasm of repudiation held her taut as the lovely taste of sensation faded, leaving only distaste in its place. She veiled her too-expressive eyes. Exactly who was waiting in the penthouse back in London for him? She was masochistically

tempted to ask but knew he would answer truthfully and
the pain would be hers, not his. And the pain away from
him, she finally acknowledged, was even greater. It didn't
matter how many other women there had been over the
past months, she still needed him, still wanted him in her
life on any terms. So perhaps it was time to match his
honesty.

'I saw you kissing Mei Ling on Dominica,' she said
abruptly.

He looked forgivably surprised by her long memory. 'I
know,' he confessed none the less.

Damp squib. An urge to thump him with the bottle of
champagne struggled within her. 'Is that all you've got to
say?'

'She launched herself at me!' The animal brilliance of his
jewelled eyes dared her to disbelieve him.

'Oh.' Claire delved back into the hamper for plates, too
self-conscious to attack such a whisper-thin explanation.
'You never said.'

'You never asked,' he answered craftily. 'Here, let me put
this stuff out. Just lie back and relax. I want an answer by
the end of the afternoon.'

'I thought you'd already made up my mind for me.'

Are you fooling him? You're not fooling yourself. Your
mind's already made up and you cast up objections,
praying he'll tear them down again. She couldn't keep on
denying herself her own heart's desire. She wasn't that
unselfish.

'I'm not a staging post in a storm. If you come back, you
stay,' he assured her arrogantly. 'And speaking as someone
who had one father and three stepfathers, there's no way
you'll ever get a divorce after the baby's born.'

Unbeknown to him, that announcement had a reassuring flavour for Claire. Obviously he wasn't regarding a
reconciliation as a trial that he could walk away from

again, and she saw how it would be. He would grant her a
corner of his life. No more, no less and she would never get
to crowd him. He wouldn't be living in the country more
than one week out of three. And Dane was a past master at
ensuring his own comfort. In any case, the baby had to be
considered. An occasional father was better than no father
at all.

'All right.' She tried not to sound too enthusiastic, but
some of it still crept out, for he searched her face suddenly.
'I don't like being on my own,' she added brightly. 'And I
like the country.'

His eyes glittered. 'I come with the package.'

'Yes, well, you'd be rather difficult to overlook,' she
replied. 'You and your ego. I hope it's a big house.' She
pillowed her cheek on the shirt he had just discarded, loving
the scent of his flesh that still clung to the fabric and stifling
a yawn. 'You know that if I clung to you and moaned and
nagged and dogged your every footstep, you'd be in
torment. You can't have it all ways.'

Impervious to his hard scrutiny, she slid into sleep, able
to wind down now that she had graciously agreed to
exactly what she wanted. He didn't let her sleep long, or so
it seemed when he woke her up, for she still felt woozy.

'Champagne.' Dane advanced, helping her upright,
finding her mules and practically putting her feet in them.
'I wonder if it's blitzed, too.'

'I only had two glasses.'

'And practically no food,' he countered. 'You'll be more
comfortable sleeping at home. The car ought to be back by
now. It's three.'

'For a mile walk?' she exclaimed, clutching his arm as the
sunlight almost blinded her. What a lovely word home was,
she reflected cheerfully, only wincing as she straightened
her back.

'For you,' he said steadily.

Ten minutes later the car was sweeping up a wooded driveway and the symmetrical splendour of Wytchwood's Georgian frontage came into view. It was not the enormous house she had feared and, tucked as it was among a grove of tall, graceful trees, it was a delightful surprise.

Thompson was opening the doors before they even reached the top of the shallow steps. His welcoming smile warmed her and she gazed appreciatively round the spacious, mosaic-tiled hall, already enchanted by the light which seemed to flood in through the tall window.

'She's too tired to take a tour,' Dane was saying with a soft laugh.

She wasn't. The drowsiness had gone, but her back remained sore so she decided it might be more sensible to lie down and rest for a while.

'You ought to go to bed.' Dane was already herding her masterfully towards the carved staircase.

'The house is lovely,' she murmured.

'Glad you like it.' He pushed open a panelled door and simultaneously a tight, clenched sensation constrained her stomach muscles and she gave a gasp of discomfort.

'What's up?' Dane demanded harshly.

She made it over to the bed before pain followed in a blinding wave, wrenching a moan of fear from her. Dane said something unprintable. As the force of the contraction receded she breathed again. 'It's the baby,' she muttered.

'Early?' He ran long fingers through his silvery hair, the gesture not far removed from one of desperation.

'Is there a hospital nearby?' she pressed anxiously.

He seemed suddenly to unfreeze and while he was out on the landing shouting for Thompson, another contraction seized her, arriving far sooner than she had naïvely expected.

Dane reappeared, to sweep her hastily off the bed. 'This is my fault. The way I carted you out of that apartment.'

'I should have realised earlier what was wrong,' she soothed uneasily. 'I never counted on this, not now . . . with you . . .'

His arms tightened round her on his passage down the stairs. 'I ought to be with you, but I won't be much help.' He gazed down at her, distinctly embarrassed. 'I'm in a cold sweat.'

For all that, he was marvellous in the car on the way to the small cottage hospital and, by the time they arrived, Claire was in no state to worry about how the experience was affecting Dane. She was swept away from him at speed and suddenly felt totally bereft, plunged at her most vulnerable into the midst of strangers.

'My goodness, that baby's not waiting for anyone!' the chirpy midwife said, and all around her there was a buzz of activity broken up by questions that she was barely able to answer, for the birth process had taken complete hold of her.

'Dane!' she cried at the peak of another powerful contraction.

'Can't you fill in your damned forms some other time?' In the interlude his whiplike drawl carried and a moment later he was there, disregarding the chilly Sister in charge's dirty look that said he was not wanted in her delivery-room. 'I want to stay.' He voiced the admission to Claire and no one else, and she grasped his hand gratefully.

They connected her to all sorts of machinery, it seemed. Someone exclaimed, 'There are two heartbeats, Sister,' which made no sense at all to Claire at the time because of course there were two, hers and the baby's.

Light was shed on the comment within half an hour. First a girl was born and then a boy. 'God, you fantastic woman!' Dane planted an extravagant kiss on her brow.

'Perhaps you'd care to wait outside now?' the Sister suggested frostily. 'While your girlfriend . . .'

'Hey, this lady's my wife,' Dane contradicted with icy hauteur and Claire managed a weak grin. He actually sounded proud of the fact.

She was all shipshape and poured into a scratchy hospital gown before she got to see him again. Exhaustion was sweeping over her now. The twins were healthy, blonde like Dane but with very dark eyes that she suspected also came from his side of the family tree. Though both babies were a little underweight, the doctor had assured her that it was quite normal in the circumstances.

Dane sank down on the edge of the bed and clasped her hand. His own was unsteady. 'I was really scared in there,' he murmured raggedly, his bright hair a damp tangle round his striking features. 'But you're OK, aren't you? Thank God . . . and them——' He paused again, a dazed aspect to his normally alert gaze, 'they're beautiful. Tiny, are they supposed to be that tiny? Hey!' He smoothed her hair off her brow almost clumsily. 'You should sleep now.'

She gave him a drowsy smile. Well, if she had failed to shake him into loving, the babies hadn't. Dane had been snared by tiny fingers and toes. She would never forget that magical look of joy on his face when they had been born. He probably wouldn't stay so enthusiastic, but she sensed it was the one bond that would never break, and one she had not hoped could exist.

'You've changed quite radically.' Carter contrived to sound peevish and reproving. 'Still, you've done very well for yourself. But I can't say I ever expected to see Dane settling down. Although with the children——' a sneer crept into his pompous voice '—he didn't have much choice, did he?'

'If I were you, I wouldn't repeat that insinuation again.' Dane's soft intervention from behind turned both their heads. His arms enclosed her teasingly, drawing her back against him firmly as he coldly surveyed Carter's flushed face. 'What is it about the Fletcher clan?' he mused. 'Even at a christening they find time to be unpleasant.'

Dane deliberately headed her away before she could add anything. 'I hate to say you were right about them but you were,' she murmured. 'With the exception of Steve, they only came to pry and bitch. Celia's been running about pricing everything. Sandra could barely bring herself to smile even at the twins!' Her breath ran out with an angered hiss.

His dazzlingly blue eyes were amused. 'Don't look now, they're leaving . . .'

'I'd better go.' His hand had already dropped from her arm which was no surprise to her. Dane rarely touched her except in public, and Matthew and Joy were seven weeks old now. Their marriage was a happy, easy-going pretence, with separate bedrooms and the separate lives that would inevitably develop from the absence of intimacy. And if anything she was more deeply in love with Dane than she had ever been. He had hugged home and hearth with unDanelike fervour of recent. He was clearly making one heck of an effort, and she wondered why she should resent him for the necessity. It was scarcely fair. He hadn't made her any promises. Colliding with his rueful smile, a drumbeat of aching tension held her tautly still until she shook hurriedly clear of the needling reminders of her own sexuality. 'And I'll check the twins, too.'

'What do we have a nanny for?'

Since Dane was often to be found at six in the morning in the nursery, getting under that same starchy nanny's feet, she just laughed. 'I haven't seen them in hours.'

'Yes, we surely have hit the jackpot on longstaying guests,' Dane breathed drily, glancing round the still crowded confines of the lounge.

She couldn't help smiling at his tone, and she took her leave of her erstwhile relatives with poise. She had much to be grateful for after all, and it wasn't being pessimistic but realistic to suspect that Dane was bound to start disappearing for long stretches soon. Squashing that apprehension irritably, she chose to survey with pride instead the difference refurnishing had made to the penthouse. Although they spent most of their time at Wytchwood, Claire had worked hard to bring a less chilly aspect to the apartment, and the warm colour schemes in the large reception-rooms were a great improvement.

Surely there was more to marriage, though, than being mother, hostess and interior decorator ... if there was, it looked as if she was destined to remain in ignorance this time around. She sighed. He liked her. He adored the twins. There was nothing cool, sophisticated or pretend about his unashamed fascination with them, and when she got to the stage where she was inclined to be envious of her own children, she knew how unreasonable she was being.

'A gentleman has called to see you, madam,' Thompson intercepted her before she reached the nursery. 'A Mr Walker. He insisted that he needed to speak to you privately. I showed him into the study.'

Claire's smooth brow furrowed. Max? What on earth would Max be doing here? Her feet carried her swiftly back down the corridor and there he was, considerably improved in apearance from their last meeting, his stocky figure complemented by a smart brown suit, his dark hair shorter and nearly combed.

He spoke the moment she entered the room, his manner almost jocular. 'You're certainly not easy to get hold of these days! Ex-directory number, out of the country half the time, and when I do finally get hold of you you're in the middle of a party,' he complained.

'Max.' Rather awkwardly she held out her hand. 'You look well.'

He clasped her fingers and held on to them. 'I must've

looked a slob that day at the flat. Fact of the matter is, things have changed. I've got a job now again, and after speaking to your cousin . . . Good lord, Claire, why didn't you tell me what you'd done that day?' he demanded heavily. 'I didn't know you were married or why until I got your cousin on the phone. He told me the whole story. I was horrified.'

Uncomfortably Claire tried to retrieve her fingers. 'My cousin?'

'Carter. When I realised what you'd done for me . . . the sacrifice . . .' He had the cheek to look insufferably smug.

Claire tugged her hand back, mentally cursing Carter. He was a pot-stirrer. He had had absolutely no business telling Max about Adam's will and embarrassing her like this. 'What sacrifice?' she asked stiffly.

'Marrying Dane. I mightn't have been able to find you but I have been reading the papers,' he confided with a covert smile. 'The guy's been running around with other women ever since you married him.'

Claire turned an angry pink. 'I fail to understnad what my marriage has to do with you, now, Max.'

'Look, Sue . . . well, I can understand you still being annoyed about that.'

'It's nothing to do with Sue,' Claire got in, in exasperation. 'Carter had no right to give you the wrong impression . . . oh, what does it matter? I happen to love Dane.'

He regarded her with irritating disbelief. 'You couldn't possibly,' he argued. 'Your cousin told me you married him to get your grandfather's money for us.'

Her mouth set. 'I'm still in love with him.'

'Sue and I are finished,' he emphasised tautly. 'Claire, I still love you.'

He grabbed both her hands as if determined to force a more encouraging response from her. She could see the anger gathering in him now, born out of the fear that he was making a fool of himself. 'We can still be together. You can get a divorce. You can't want to stay with him . . .' he beseeched roughly. 'You don't know how much I've regretted hurting you and how much I've missed you.'

A rush of moisture stung her eyelids. She hated to hurt anybody. Perhaps only loneliness and boredom had been behind Max's involvement with Sue, but it was irrelevant now. His appearance here was only an embarrassment now for both of them. 'Max,' she interrupted tightly, a tiny shake in her voice. 'Dane and I have children. I'm sorry . . . I . . .'

Max suddenly loosed her hands and backed off. Abstractedly she turned her head to see what had stolen his attention from her.

CHAPTER TEN

'You've got guests to take care of,' Dane murmured with a brilliant and quite terrifying smile. 'Though I do hate to break up such a touching scene.'

The blaze of fury in his sapphire eyes was visible only for a second before his thick lashes cloaked their expressiveness. 'Move, Claire,' he added softly.

And leave Max to his tender mercies? Was he joking? Hot-cheeked, she bit her lip, unable to understand why he was so angry. 'I'll just see Max out,' she dared.

For a moment she thought he was going to object. He flung Max, who was standing behind her, a cruelly amused appraisal. 'I wasn't going to lay a finger on him, Claire!' And with that, he swung on his heel.

'Does he usually talk to you like that?' Max muttered, fiddling with his collar as if it was strangling him.

'When he's angry ... he——' Distressed by Dane's behaviour, she spun again. 'I'm sorry. You'd better go. I do wish you well, but ...'

'He doesn't love you,' Max jeered, reacting to what he read in her eloquent face. 'He just looked at you like you crawled out from under a stone. He's a decadent, womanising ...'

'I might have liked you better if you'd said that to his face,' Claire retorted crushingly.

Max departed in high dudgeon in the wake of several other guests. If Carter hadn't already gone, Claire would have given him a piece of her mind. Balked of her prey, infuriated with Dane, she stayed out of his path none the less. Why should she throw Max out, just for visiting? Dane had probably slept with a dozen different women during their separation and—why didn't she face it?—since their reconciliation. His sexual uninterest in his wife was self-explanatory. He was clearly finding physical satisfaction outside their relationship, and she'd been cravenly burying her head in the sand sooner than meet that sordid truth head on.

Ironically, Max's hypocritical comments on Dane's reputation had plunged her back to hard reality. Dane had chipped away at her self-respect until she had no backbone left at all. She loved him more than it was healthy to love anybody. Perhaps it was sick of her to have compromised to such an extent.

Dane appeared to be politely ignoring her when she returned to the party. It was Randy who hissed in her ear. 'What's wrong with Dane?'

'Nothing,' Claire murmured tautly.

'Gil said he's furious about something,' her friend confided rather tipsily. 'Not that I can see it. He's smiling.'

Why should he be furious? She hadn't asked Max to come! But Dane still believed she loved Max—the admission slunk into her disordered thoughts. She had never disabused him of the notion. He had never brought it up. She shot a less defiant glance down to the foot of the room where Dane was calmly chatting to friends. How much of their conversation had he heard?

The last of their guests departed mid-evening in a sudden, dismaying clump. Claire headed away from the hall at a steady rate of knots. A hand fell on her shoulder and spun her back.

'Going somewhere? If it's your bedroom, I'll join you. But first——' Dane enunicated shortly, his supple hands easing slowly down over her taut spinal cord to cup the swell of her hips and weld her intimately into the hard cradle of his thighs, bringing her into full, forceful contact with his rawly masculine body. 'This.'

Caught totally by surprise, her own body's needs and wants rushed uncontrollably to the fore when he drove her lips apart with a hard, very sexually orientated kiss. His effect on her after so long was explosive. He lifted his silvery head and she read the purpose in the hot glitter of his eyes. Shock winged through her in waves. She was shaking all over, a gnawing ache of need she despised now, making its dissatisfaction felt inside her.

'I was going to wait for ever if I was going to wait for an invitation,' he said roughly. 'What was he doing here?'

Trying jerkily to detach herself from his fierce hold, she snapped, 'It was just a social call.'

'Like hell it was a social call!' You standing there weeping apology for the trap you were in, mumbling about the twins like they had a stranglehold on you!' Dane gritted, smouldering down into the flushed triangle of her now bemused face. 'If you go, you go without them, but if you stay, you share my bed. I'm damned if I'm putting up with this any longer. Maybe it's time you remembered that you're my wife and that wives have certain obligations . . .'

'No,' Claire said flatly, unequivocally. As she understood his intent, a seething, bitter anger was rising tempestuously within her slim frame. Dane was never again going to use sex to subjugate her with, and that was evidently his aim. It stung his pride that Max had come here and that she had seemed upset. She couldn't forget how indifferent Dane had been to her physical attractions out in the Caribbean or since their reconciliation. It was a base insult for him to invite her to his bed now, and a tragic irony that had he invited her yesterday or the day before she would have fallen eagerly into his arms, convinced their marriage finally had a future. But not this way, not when he was angry and his desire was motivated purely by the lowering suspicion that his homely little wife might actually still prefer another man to him.

'And my goodness, things must be getting desperate when you have to come down to making a move on me!' she threw in helpless bitterness. Even the sound of her own sharpened voice pained. She sounded all that she despised in herself. A violently jealous and insecure wife.

'Claire,' Dane breathed.

'I prefer things the way they are,' she interrupted shakily. 'It's healthier.'

'Excuse me, Mr ... Mrs Visconti.' Their nanny's icy, rigidly disapproving voice fell into the pool of silence. Dane's arms dropped from her but the cold threat in his eyes hadn't dwindled.

Before he could utter a further upsetting word, Claire took advantage of their audience to flee, crimson-faced, to her room. She turned the key in the lock and hurled herself on the bed. Right at this moment she hated him for being capable of making love to her only out of anger, when she had been pathetically suppressing her own need for him every hour of every day and telling herself that she could cope with a platonic marriage as long as he still lived with her.

'Open this door, Claire!' The brass handle rattled.

'Get lost,' she mumbled into the pillow. If only he'd been jealous. She had forgotten how cruel Dane could be and how damnably unpredictable. She had forgotten that he looked on her as a possession, and she was suddenly so grateful that he didn't know that she loved him. That was the one defence that enabled her to stand up to him. Shorn of it, Dane would get away with murder.

There was an awesome crash and a splintering squeal as

the door crashed back drunkenly on its hinges, framing Dane on the threshold. 'Don't you ever lock a door against me again!' he warned.

The atmosphere was explosive. Claire coiled back cravenly against the headboard. For the count of ten soul-destroying seconds, Dane studied her. An expression of angry distaste hardened his bronzed features. 'You want him that badly, go to him,' he said very quietly. 'I'm an ungrateful bastard, aren't I? You didn't put a foot wrong with him. You told him you were in love with me. You'd stay because you promised me you'd stay, and for the twins. And the only damned thing you can't control is your response to me sexually and you're terrified of that now. It doesn't go with the martyred image.'

His first words literally paralysed her. A confrontation that frankly petrified her had sprung up out of nowhere. Dane was inviting her to leave. 'Dane, you ... you misunderstood.'

He stared at her with unholy contempt. 'Oh, I haven't misunderstood anything,' he contradicted savagely. 'Until Max showed today I actually thought things were good between us. But what the hell, you can lie back and think about another guy in anybody's bed as long as it's not mine. The little jerk wasn't even faithful to you. Whereas I was goddamned crazy enough to subject myself to a year of celibacy! Well, that's at an end. You can do whatever the blue blazes you like, Claire, but I'm getting laid tonight by a warm, willing woman!'

His candid promise sent her off the bed like an electrified eel. 'You do that and you needn't bother coming home! Do you ...?' Her lips worked convulsively, her brain working on reverse mode. 'A year of celibacy,' she whispered dazedly. 'Dane, I don't love Max!'

But she was talking to thin air. She heard Thompson at

his most expressionless, saying, 'Shall I contact a joiner in the morning, sir?'

Where he got the nerve to rebuke Dane in the mood he was in, she could not begin to guess and Dane's reply was masked by the sob of her own tortured breathing. In the space of an evening their carefully rebuilt relationship had fallen apart at the seams. She had let her emotions overpower her judgement. She had hugged her pride zealously to herself and called it self-respect. What kind of marriage had she expected to have when she had let Dane believe that she still loved Max? It didn't matter that he didn't love her. He had always been honest. She hadn't been. She had been hiding behind the truth as if it was something to be ashamed of, and in doing so she had driven Dane away.

It took her thirty seconds to reach the front door, but the lift had already gone. By the time it got back and she got down to the underground car park there was only a curious security guard in view and Dane's Ferrari was gone. Distraught she hurried back into the lift.

He had actually heard her telling Max that she loved him and he hadn't believed it. In dismay she saw the barrier she herself had raised between them. Dane had been very unlikely to make love to her while he imgained she was dreaming of another man . . . only in anger had he turned to express his dissatisfaction, his frustration. Yet to credit that there had been no other women for him all these months in addition, demanded, to her mind, a degree of certifiable insanity. Dane had thought she was living with Max.

If Dane went to someone else tonight, she had only herself to thank. Her stupid pride had ruined everything. In her room she got ready for bed. Whatever he did tonight was her fault. She wouldn't hold it against him. It was time

she practised honesty with him even if it hurt. After driving
herself half-way to distraction imagining where he might
be, she went in to look at the twins.

In the dim glow of the nightlight it was Dane's tall, lean
figure she focused on first. He was tucking Matthew back
into his cot. Her breath snarled up in her throat in a tide of
aching relief. 'When did you get back?' she asked
prosaically.

'I got to the end of the block and I came back just in time
to see our nanny packed and departing.' He shot her a
curiously evasive glance. 'Seems she told Thompson she
wasn't staying in a household lacking in moral tone. It must
have been the door and the fight that riled her. You can
blame me. I started it all.'

'I didn't like her very much anyway,' Claire answered
without a moment's hesitation. 'I'd prefer someone younger
and not so regimented.'

'Thompson's already mentioned a niece. He was
mortally offended by the suggestion that we lacked moral
tone.' Dane's dark-timbred drawl trembled revealingly,
and then steadied when he gazed down at her anxious face.
His hand curved over her shoulder, inexorably guiding her
towards the door. 'You know, I was talking to Matthew
before you came in. He makes a great uncritical audience
but he couldn't seem to think of a face-saving excuse for me
only getting to the end of the block, either.' He thrust open
his own bedroom door. 'We've got to talk and Thompson's
still rustling about the lounge.'

She lodged awkwardly in the centre of the carpet and
gave up on the eye-to-eye contact, recognising its inhibiting
effect on her ability to articulate. 'I should have told you
ages ago . . .' she began.

'If you're about to apologise for something, I may just
strangle you,' he interrupted ruefully. 'I came on to you like

a sex starved adolescent tonight. I just lost my head when I saw you with him. I couldn't stomach the idea that you wanted to be with him instead of me. It sounds pretty damned childish.' He gave a ragged sigh. 'But it didn't feel childish at the time. I didn't feel at all grateful for the fact you were lying to him because that was the right thing to do. Mind you, if you'd encouraged him I'd have thrown him down the lift shaft. What I'm trying to say, not very well . . . is that I'm sorry.'

He was eyeing her levelly when she looked up, still reeling from the apology. 'I didn't encourage him because . . .'

'Because you wouldn't behave that way,' Dane cut in on her again, his mouth sardonically set. 'You're too loyal.'

And dull as ditchwater, she almost added. He was being so logical in explaining exactly why he had behaved as he had, and he wouldn't let her get a word in edgeways because he was presupposing her replies in that maddening fashion of his.

'You're not thinking of going anywhere, are you?'

Claire shook her head in dismay.

Dane actually smiled. 'If I'd gone for him, you'd have been all over him like a rash. I'm not that dumb,' he reflected cheerfully. 'He won't be here again, will he?'

Again she shook her head, rather flummoxed by his calm. 'I love you.' It came out as a mutter rather than a dignified announcement.

Dane was surveying her almost absently. 'Do you know what hit me at the end of the block? That you might go. I haven't given you enough time, but it's a hell of a strain living with you and not touching you. Maybe I should have made that clearer sooner, but when I got you back I didn't much care how I did it,' he admitted, studying a point to the left of her. It sank into her then that not only had he not heard what she had said but that he wasn't demonstrating calm but uncertainty of her response.

She took a deep breath. 'I love you, so I don't know what you're worrying about me leaving for. I love you quite obsessively really. I can't bear you out of my sight.' A rueful little giggle escaped her dried lips. 'I should have told you a long time ago and then you wouldn't have misunderstood about Max, but I didn't want you feeling sorry for me and then ... later, well, it was pride,' she completed simply.

She had got through this time. Although he hadn't moved he was looking directly at her. 'Well, you could say something,' she continued in a stiff little voice that concealed her hurt. 'I don't expect you to love me back, but we have other things ...' The jerky flow of her words came to a halt under the shockingly uncool onslaught of Dane's heated scrutiny.

'How long have you been in love with me?' he demanded as he yanked her bodily into his arms, crushing her breasts against the hard wall of his chest.

'Probably most of my life!' She attempted a watery smile. 'Only I didn't realise I hadn't got over you until we were on Dominica. I think I was fond of Max, and of course I was lonely.'

'You were telling him the truth tonight when you said you loved me?' he prompted, not quite levelly. His long fingers framed her cheekbones fiercely, painfully.

'Yes.'

'You crazy woman!' There was a laugh and a twisted agony in his hoarsened voice as he gave her a little shake. 'Don't you know how I feel about you? Do I have to hire the Red Arrows to blaze it in the sky? God knows, everybody else knows! I love you. If I hadn't loved you I wouldn't have bullied you into coming back,' he breathed roughly. 'Your pregnancy gave me all the ammunition I needed. I had a line of tearjerking arguments I didn't even get to use because you agreed. If you'd forced me to the last ditch, I'd have told you I loved you then.'

His hold on her was so tight her ribs hurt. She made no complaint. Had she died and gone to heaven she could not have been more devastated. A vaguely floaty feeling was interfering with her thought processes. 'You really missed me after I left Dominica?' she pressed.

He groaned, lifting her easily up in his arms and folding her down with him in a comfortable heap on the bed. 'I realised I loved you the day you were ill. It tore me inside out watching you cry. I'd been telling myself I was just fond of you ever since I brought you down to London, and there were so many things I blanked out. That morning at the Dorchester when you were in bed——' He half-smiled. 'I was trying to work out how you could look so sexy in that ghastly nightgown and then I didn't like the way I was thinking so I got out. So when I went to bed with you I was really just giving myself the excuse to do what I wanted to do deep down inside, and then I couldn't keep away from you. I was always possessive of you,' he murmured ruefully. 'I never questioned that until you talked blithely about moving in with another man and I didn't like the idea.'

Claire looked up at him dazedly. 'But you asked me about Max that day, you told me . . .'

'I was flattened when I saw those bloody photos. I guess in a way it was funny. I deserved it. But I'd promised myself that after all the damage I'd done, I'd put everything right again for you if I could,' he confessed tautly. 'And if you wanted Max, then I didn't have any right to foul that up again. I nearly went out of my mind when I thought you were living with him.'

Her tongue suddenly unglued from the roof of her mouth. 'But you let me go. You even smiled at me when you saw me on to the plane!'

'I thought you loved him, and I had spent all that time on Dominica trying to court you.' A winged brow elevated at the old-fashioned term. 'But, dammit, I didn't get anywhere with you.'

Claire, who had never played the temptress in her life, was busy unbuttoning his shirt. Her fingers were clumsy at her self-appointed task, but he didn't seem to notice.

'Everything I did on Dominica seemed to turn out wrong.' Lines of strain grooved between his narrow-bridged nose and hardened mouth as he relived his frustration then. 'Hell, I didn't know . . . don't know the first thing about showing a woman I love her. I didn't want to scare you again so I gave you space, but you couldn't even bear me to touch you . . . and that hurt,' he confided. 'That hurt one hell of a lot because I wasn't trying to get you into bed. I did learn one lesson early on. You had to care about me first or it was going to be the hairshirt and the mute look of distaste at dawn again.'

'That night on the beach you pushed me away, . . .'

'I thought all I was getting offered was sex. You're one heck of a good actress. You were friendly but you were distant. Hey . . .' A furrow carved between his brows as he gazed down at her. 'What are you doing?'

'What do you think?' Set free of her own insecurities, Claire was bent on indulging every fantasy she had ever had on her long, lonely nights over the past year. She was fingering through a mental array of erotic possibilities when what came naturally took over. Turning her lips against the fast beat of his heart, the tip of her tongue teased a path through the dark, curling hair smattering his chest to a flat, male nipple.

'Oh, God . . .' Dane went satisfyingly rigid. Probably with shock, she allowed, her hand sliding caressingly over his flat stomach, swiftly followed by her mouth. A long shudder racked his lean, exquisite male frame and she embarked on his belt buckle with heightened courage.

'You don't have to do this.' Claire clashed with bright, anxious eyes and the storm of desire he couldn't hide there. He lost his immobility when her wandering hands smoothed slowly up over his taut thigh muscles. 'You're right, we do.' He caved in by tugging her down on top of him. That's the first time you've ever encouraged me!' and there was wonderment in his husky drawl.

His brilliant eyes clung to hers for a split, mindblowing second before his hands cupped her breasts and his mouth took hers with a sudden fierce urgency. A soft moan broke low in her throat, and he needed no further invitation. Clothes were discarded in haste and all the time he kept on kissing her and her temperature kept on shooting higher, the excitement exploding between them, uncontrolled and intense.

It wasn't an orchestrated seduction. It happened so fast. He entered her with a single compelling thrust and the world splintered around her simultaneously. Dane gave a groan of wondering pleasure that she would have echoed had she had the oxygen. It made her feel the most desirable woman on earth, and then the glorious all-encompassing power of his lovemaking consigned every remaining thought into oblivion.

'I feel so good.'

He grinned. 'No need to sound so surprised.'

'I feel like I could fly.'

'Not without me!' Dane propped himself on his elbow and just stared at her, everything he'd never permitted her to see before brimming in his jewelled eyes. 'This is happy,' he muttered half under his breath, and her eyes swam with tears and she just held him the way she'd always wanted to hold him.

'You should never have let me leave Dominica,' she complained unsteadily.

'Shoot, Claire, that was the most unselfish thing I ever did in my entire life!' Bleak humour glittered beneath his luxuriant lashes. 'It made me feel good for all of an hour. I'm not very good at being patient.'

In the Caribbean she had traced his every move back to an over active conscience. That modest misconception had become an impregnable barrier, and how nearly they had lost each other completely! Dane gently stroked her hair back from her brows. 'You see, I hoped you might find out Max wasn't to your taste after all, and when you never wrote to Lew demanding a divorce, my hopes started to rise. I couldn't picture you living happily in sin, but Claire, don't ever make me jealous again,' he urged with shadowy self-mockery. 'Jealousy is hell. Thinking of you being with him all those months.'

She pressed her lips against his smooth shoulder. 'I'm sorry. I didn't know.' She swallowed. 'Was there anyone else?'

'I didn't want anyone else,' Dane told her firmly. 'Five-foot-one-inch redheads with giant-sized inferiority complexes don't exactly strew every corner. I wanted you and only you.'

He looked so fantastically good-looking and sexy, she treated him to a slightly pole-axed smile, euphoria flowing through her in an ecstatic tide of acceptance. He really was hers, all hers.

'And Mei Ling . . .' He threaded fingers through her silky hair ruefully. 'I didn't exactly push her away when I heard you coming. I brought her to the house deliberately. I wanted to see if it bothered you. No . . . you're right, it wasn't the cleverest stunt I ever pulled.'

Her fingers skated suggestively down over his lean ribcage. 'Next time I catch you being pawed ...'

'I'm reformed.' He dealt her a look that just dared the smallest cloud of distrust.

'And just like the carpet and the sheets on the bed you belong to me, right?'

'What did I say about your self-confidence?' He rested back, sleek and tawny against the pillows, sheer provocation cloaked in human flesh. 'I didn't even get to grovel tonight. I was going to.'

'I love you.'

'Keep on saying it.' His arms tightened round her and he started to kiss her again. She made a mental note to tell her daughter when she grew up that fantasies did occasionally come true.

Winner of the
Romance Writers of America
Golden Medallion Award

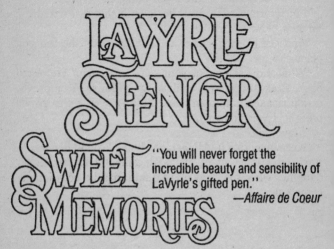

LAVYRLE SPENCER

SWEET MEMORIES

"You will never forget the
incredible beauty and sensibility of
LaVyrle's gifted pen."
—*Affaire de Coeur*

A celebration of courage, fulfillment and fiery love . . . every
woman's story, every woman's dream.

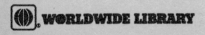 **WORLDWIDE LIBRARY**

SWT-1

ATTRACTIVE, SPACE SAVING BOOK RACK

Display your most prized novels on this handsome and sturdy book rack. The hand-rubbed walnut finish will blend into your library decor with quiet elegance, providing a practical organizer for your favorite hard-or soft-covered books.

Only $9.95

Approximately 16" x 8" when assembled

Assembles in seconds!

To order, rush your name, address and zip code, along with a check or money order for $10.70* ($9.95 plus 75¢ postage and handling) payable to *Harlequin Reader Service*:

Harlequin Reader Service
Book Rack Offer
901 Fuhrmann Blvd.
P.O. Box 1396
Buffalo, NY 14269-1396

Offer not available in Canada.

*New York and Iowa residents add appropriate sales tax.

BKR-1A

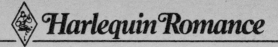
Coming Next Month

2917 THE HEALING EFFECT Deborah Davis
Raine can't abandon young Stevie when his mother dies in the car crash. But not until Dr. Kyle Benedict begins to show equal concern does she think about the really eye-opening consequences of becoming involved—with Stevie and the doctor.

2918 AN UNLIKELY COMBINATION
Anne Marie Duquette
Sherri Landers is the most competent ranger on the isolated Colorado mountain station. And the loneliest. Until she's paired with one M. S. Barrett, a man whose reputation for daring rescues—and unspeakable behavior—matches her own.

2919 A STAR FOR A RING Kay Gregory
Crysten's world turns upside down when businessman Gregg Malleson kisses her—not just because he's attractive, but because she suddenly, disturbingly remembers where she'd met him before!

2920 MAN OF SHADOWS Kate Walker
From their first meeting Madeleine knows that Jordan Sumner is the special man in her life. Yet how can she win his love when he is so embittered by some secret of the past—one he refuses to even discuss?

2921 FORTUNE'S FOOL Angela Wells
Just graduated from convent school, Ria is determined not to submit to the arrogant Brazilian who kidnaps her on her way to join her guardian. But Vitor Fortunato wants revenge, and he isn't going to let this opportunity slip out of his hands....

2922 BID FOR INDEPENDENCE Yvonne Whittal
Wealthy Maura Fielding doesn't need to work, but she's determined to be a teacher and live a normal life. She can't understand why her stepbrother, Clayton, is so opposed. After all, she's an adult now, free to choose.

Available in July wherever paperback books are sold, or through Harlequin Reader Service:

In the U.S.
901 Fuhrmann Blvd.
P.O. Box 1397
Buffalo, N.Y. 14240-1397

In Canada
P.O. Box 603
Fort Erie, Ontario
L2A 5X3

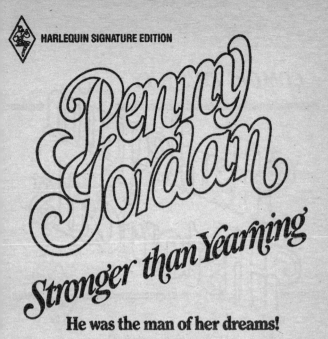

COMING THIS JULY

Storytelling at its best
by some of your favorite authors such as
Kristen James, Nora Roberts, Cassie Edwards

Strong, independent heroines
Heroes you'll fall in love with
Compelling love stories

History has never been so romantic.

Look for them in July wherever Harlequin Books are sold.